BLESS your HEART

VALENTINE TEXAS BOOK ONE

LYRA PARISH

Copyright © 2023 Lyra Parish
www.lyraparish.com

Bless Your Heart
Valentine Texas, #1

Cover Designer: Dee Garcia, Black Widow Designs
Photographer: Wander Aguiar
Cover Model: Lachy
Editor: Jenny Sims, Editing 4 Indies
Proofreader: Amanda Cuff, Word of Advice Editing

This one's for you, Dad.
You taught me that if I fall out of the saddle, always
get back on, and I know you'd be proud of me for not
quitting. As you always said—at least you showed.
Rest easy, cowboy.

AUTHOR'S NOTE

This is the first book I've released solo since 2016. A lot has changed in my life since then, but one thing has stayed the same—me writing romance. I'm so dang grateful that you chose to read Bless Your Heart when you have thousands (dare I say millions) of other romance books to choose from. Thank you for giving me a chance. I love writing small-town southern romance because it feels like home, and I hope you feel the same reading it. I appreciate you so much, and I can never say thank you enough. Happy Reading!

XO
   Lyra Parish

I ONCE BELIEVED LOVE WOULD BE BURNING RED. BUT IT'S GOLDEN.

—TAYLOR SWIFT

1

SUMMER

"*S*hit," I mutter, rolling over and turning off the alarm screaming for me to get my ass out of bed. It's half past six, and I stayed up way too late last night swiping the cringy men away on the dating app my best friend, Kinsley, forced me to download. I wasn't even remotely attracted to *one* guy on there. Over the past few months, I've given this app my best try. I've even gone on several awkward-as-hell dates. Chivalry is Dead Shawn, Handsy Henry, and Bad Breath Bart had me drowning myself in a huge tub of mint chocolate chip ice cream before midnight. Don't even get me started on Farting Frank. Each time he coughed, he let one rip, and I reconsidered my life choices. Everyone talks a big game about finding dates online, but I've had zero hookups or booty calls, just a handful of bad experiences.

At this point, I'm convinced that I'll be single forever with a barn full of horses, some chickens, and goats…just because they're cute. Maybe I'll never be able to live out my dream of being a MILF business owner with a hot as hell husband. Nope, just a lonely old woman who collects animals like postage stamps. But at least I've got a nice ass, a great smile, and a sense of humor. Sometimes my sassy mouth gets me in trouble.

1

After dressing, I slip on my boots and head outside. Working on a ranch means getting up at the butt crack of dawn, and it being the weekend doesn't matter. I check the plants on my porch—yep, still dead—then walk across the pasture toward the chicken coop.

Cluck. Cluck. Cluck.

"Hey, ladies." I enter with a big smile on my face. Some are roosting, while others are foraging for early-morning worms. I grab a pail of feed and throw it out by the handful. The hens rush over, pecking at the seed on the ground. They scatter around me, clucking away, and I love how happy they are. Happy chickens mean yummy eggs, and you can't beat free-range eggs from chickens you raised yourself.

"Have a good day, chickadees." I make my way toward the big red barn, where most of the horses used for ranch duties are housed. My family owns the Lazy J, but nothing is lazy about it when it comes to raising and trading cattle. The three-thousand-acre property has been in my family for several generations. But honestly, that's the case for most who reside in Valentine, Texas. It's the norm around here.

The West Texas mountains surround the prairie lands where Valentine is located, and it's a true Southern oasis. Our town isn't big, but we have the essentials—a grocery store, bakery, café, bank, and even a plant nursery. We have the essentials that make living in the middle of nowhere a bit easier. There are a few locally owned restaurants and antique shops, but there's nothing like what one would expect to find in a bigger city. However, this is home, a place where everyone knows everyone's business and one another. You might even miss it if you're driving down Highway 90 and blink.

"Good mornin'." My dad looks over his shoulder at me as he saddles up Sassy. She's a deep red quarter horse that loves to gallop. He's wearing his old straw cowboy hat with grease stains from working on tractors and his trusty cowboy boots. His mustache is curled at the ends, and he smiles.

"Mornin'. Where ya headin' off to?"

His blue eyes meet mine. "Gonna go check the water well across the property by the east side. One of the ranch hands mentioned the pressure bein' low, so I'm goin' to check it out while I got some time."

"Wouldn't a four-wheeler be faster?"

He slides his worn boot into the stirrup, and he pulls himself into the old leather western saddle seat. It's Daddy's favorite saddle, with sterling silver embellishments and an intricate design carved into it.

"It's just not the cowboy way." He shoots me a wink and takes off. I give him a wave and continue with my morning duties.

By the time I return home to grab a late breakfast, I have four texts from Kinsley.

> Call me.
>
> I know you feel this vibrating in your back pocket.
>
> Bump?

I laugh at that one.

> I'm driving to your house. It's an emergency!

Before I can respond, I hear someone blaring a horn outside. I walk out, and Kinsley hops out of her truck.

"Someone better be dyin'." I'm not used to seeing her midmorning like this, but she looks put together. She scrunches her button nose and laughs as she tucks dark brown hair behind her ear. We may be complete opposites, but we look like we could be sisters. Growing up, we used to tell people who didn't know us that we were.

"No, but *you* might after I fill you in on the news."

I make a face, not particularly liking the sound of that. "Should I be excited or pissed?"

"Excited." She lifts a brow.

One thing about Kinsley is she knows *everything* that's going on in our small town. Valentine isn't large, but it's full of drama, and usually, we live for it. Unless it involves us.

I impatiently wait a few more seconds. "Kins! Are ya gonna make me beg? Geez, spill it!"

She's overly giddy. "Nah, I think I want to let ya guess."

"You're pregnant." I don't even wait a beat before I say it.

She glares at me, offended. "I don't *even* think so."

"Oh yeah, totally forgot ya kinda had to be doin' it with someone for that to happen."

"Who says I'm not doin' it?" She laughs.

I wave her inside. "Want some coffee?"

"Yeah, I'll take a cup, but I gotta head back to work, so I can't stay long. What's your second guess?"

I look at her over my shoulder. "Hayden's movin' back to town."

"We don't talk about him," Kinsley snaps. "He better not show his face in Valentine ever again."

Hayden Shaw was Kinsley's high school sweetheart who she thought she'd marry one day. Now he's public enemy number one, the ex-boyfriend she pretends doesn't exist. The last I heard, he quickly got engaged to the woman he started dating after Kinsley, but they still haven't planned the wedding. Or at least his mama keeps telling me that.

"One more guess." She grabs the steaming hot mug from me. I set a bottle of vanilla creamer onto the counter, and she pours it in.

"I give up! Just tell me!" I stir some cream in mine and take a small sip. A smile immediately touches my lips because it tastes like happiness in a cup.

"The Horseshoe Creek Ranch is goin' up for sale later this week."

My mouth falls open. "What? How did you find out? Are the Whitleys okay?"

She looks at her nails. "Oh yeah, they're totally fine. Their granddaughter Natalie contacted the newspaper just an hour ago sayin' she wanted to run a local ad before officially putting it on the market."

"Do you know why?" Properties on this side of town rarely go up for sale, so this is huge news. Nothing so close to my parents' place has been on the market for as long as I've been alive. Especially not right next door.

"Apparently, they want to move to a retirement community in Florida. Be closer to their kids, grandkids, and soon-to-be great-grandchildren. Plus, being a short way from major hospitals and airports are important to them. I think she said Mr. Whitley was eighty-two now."

My mouth falls open. "Wow. I think I'm in shock." I sit on one of the stools next to Kinsley and stare at my coffee. "Did they say how much?"

"No, she didn't. Mentioned somethin' 'bout doin' closed offers. But I had to tell you because *this* is your opportunity, Summer. I know you've been talkin' 'bout opening that damn bed-and-breakfast since we were kids. You made me eat a million pancakes and waffles until you perfected them. The Whitley house is huge. It's a perfect size. Not to mention the property is right next door to your parents."

"It would be incredible." I think about opening a relaxing ranch retreat for people who want to escape the hustle and bustle of their everyday lives. Everything she said is true. The location is ideal, too.

"Okay, what's the frown for?" She holds her mug between her hands.

"I don't know if I can afford it. Seems like a pipe dream."

"They said they're willing to take any and *all* reasonable offers from locals whose families have been here for generations. The Whitleys love you."

"Okay, but that doesn't solve my money problem."

"I'd bet my left tit that your parents would loan you some cash, and I know you've been saving every penny you've ever earned for this very moment. Can always take a loan. If you opened a B&B here, it would do so well. The hotel above the general store just can't accommodate people for all the hometown festivals anymore."

I grow giddy imagining the bed-and-breakfast becoming a reality.

"That's what I like to see." Kinsley grins. "That ranch is meant to be yours. Oh, before I forget, the ad is gonna run on Wednesday, but I can contact Natalie and see if you can make an offer before everyone else."

"That would be amazin'." I glance over at her. "Do you think anyone else would be interested in buyin' it?"

She shrugs. "Not that I know of. Can't think of a single soul."

"Not even your parents? I ask because the Horseshoe Creek Ranch splits our families' ranches. Ya know, sometimes people like to expand."

"Doubt it." She drinks half of her coffee in one big gulp. "Dad has already said five thousand acres is plenty. His words, not mine."

I squeal, unable to contain it anymore.

"Just gotta promise me that if for some reason Mr. Anderson ever fires me from the newspaper for bein' a little too risqué, you'll hire me."

A snort escapes me, and I hold out my hand. When she grabs it, we shake on it. "That's a deal."

"Great. You know that ole curmudgeon ain't ever gonna pull that corncob outta his ass. I'm already on thin ice. He needs to get laid."

I nearly choke on the sip of coffee I was drinking. "Kinsley!"

"What? It's true. He's too uptight and doesn't understand

that news don't spread like it did in the 1920s. Social media is a thang. News articles bein' posted online is normal. He hates computers!"

"Don't you dare get fired. We'll never hear all the juicy gossip again. Your thumb is on the pulse."

"Right? I'm basically the local therapist at this point. Did you know Lucy, the librarian, is sleepin' with the barber?"

My eyes go wide. "Seriously? What's his nickname? Hogleg?"

"Yep! Her asshole husband doesn't even know." Kinsley tilts her head. "And I ain't tellin' him either. He's a jerk."

"How do you know they're bangin'?" I meet her gaze over my mug, which is nearly empty now.

"Saw them together. Lucy about shit her pants when I found them in the stacks with his hand down her skirt. Also, you know that man doesn't read anything but tractor manuals. He's not foolin' anyone, especially not me."

"I cannot believe this. One day, you should write a book about the small-town drama."

She snickers. "No one would believe it's half-true."

"Except every person in Valentine."

Kinsley stands, rinses her mug, then sets it into the sink. "It'd be a bestseller. I'd name it…*Spill the Sweet Tea*." She turns around, beaming.

"Oh my God, that's an amazin' title. You have to do it. Or at least start an anonymous blog. You could be the Lady Whistledown of Valentine. Can you imagine?"

"Hmm. Maybe. That'd be fun, wouldn't it? But it ain't gonna pay the bills, and if my boss found out, he'd probably fire my ass!"

"You could always become a detective or somethin'. Solvin' crimes. Murders and mysteries."

"In Valentine? The only crime I've ever seen is men wearin' white knee socks with shorts."

I burst into laughter because she's not wrong.

7

She smirks and pretends to dust off her shoulder. "I'll make some phone calls and keep you updated. It's yours, babe! Putting it into the universe for you so *all* the magic will happen." She stands and sets her mug into the sink, then I walk her out. Kinsley bends over and looks at the plants on my porch.

"Are you feedin' these things poison? Jesus."

I groan. "No! I'm giving them nutrients and water, just like Vera said. I even made sure they get plenty of sun during the day."

"Well, I don't think this is what my little sister had in mind." She shakes her head, touching the pitiful leaves, then stands upright. "They make fake plants, ya know?"

"Hush! Oh, while you're speaking to that magical universe of yours, can you also tell it to send me a man? Preferably tall, handsome, older, mature, with no baggage or terrible addictions."

She gives me a look, knowing I'm not very woo-woo. However, she believes in all that stuff, and maybe it will work this time. Basically, I'm desperate.

"I'm takin' it the dating app didn't work out?"

"Hell no. I think every man I matched with was a total weirdo. One asked me if I'd consider not shaving my armpits for a month, then letting him…I can't even continue. It was a lot."

"Eww. Maybe you're a weirdo magnet."

I playfully swat at her, but she's too fast, and I miss her. "Honestly, I hate it when that happens. But they say thirty is the new twenty, so I'm not givin' up hope for us." Kinsley climbs into her truck and gives me her signature smirk.

"I hope you're right. Otherwise, I might not get married until I'm fifty!"

She snickers. "I guess if all else fails, you could always marry my brother."

"Which one?" I glare at her.

8

"Whichever one you want, considerin' I've got five to choose from. But I know exactly which one you'd match with…*if* you had to."

I roll my eyes. "I'd rather be single for life than to *ever* go on a date with Beckett."

She pops her truck into reverse and speaks to me out of the window. "Whatever you say! Not foolin' me, though." She waves and takes off. I watch her slowly travel down my driveway and turn onto the old country road that leads to town.

Kinsley's family is huge—she has five brothers and four sisters, and all the Valentine kids range from the ages of sixteen to thirty-two. I always envied that. However, I've also always felt like the eleventh kid in their family. Her parents are like my own, and they've never treated me any differently.

One summer, her mom had the nerve to ground me, along with Kinsley, for stealing horses. We've been thick as thieves since kindergarten, and I've had a vendetta against her older brother since I was fourteen. But the hatred started in high school.

Beckett has always purposely dug his roots under my skin. He's the epitome of an alphahole. He can have whoever he wants, whenever he wants, and that person has *never* been me.

The *only* reason Kinsley offers him as bait is for personal gain. For as long as I can remember, she's always wanted me to be her sister, and he's the only one I've ever been attracted to. Beckett is six-two, with muscles that ripple down his body from all the horse training and riding lessons he's given. He has the same blue eyes that all the Valentines have. Freckles sprinkle across his nose, and don't even get me started on the tattoos he's gotten over the years. His light-brown hair is always a mess, which he hides under cowboy hats or baseball caps. Scruff lines his chiseled jaw. When he offers a smile with his perfectly plump lips and perfectly straight teeth, it's enough to bring any woman to her knees. Basically, he's Southern sex on legs and can be charming when he wants, which isn't often. Not to mention, out of all five of her brothers, he's the only one who's older. Younger men aren't my thing.

That said, I'd rather eat a bag of rocks than be around him in any capacity. Beckett has always argued with me over the stupidest things. Since we were kids, he's done everything he could to annoy me, and even though we're older, that hasn't stopped. If there is an opportunity for a low blow, he takes it every single time. And the fact that I crushed on him when I was fourteen doesn't mean shit. Beckett Valentine can fuck straight off. I *hate* him and hate that the devil is so damn gorgeous.

I return inside and grab a few farm-fresh eggs, cheese, bacon, and a skillet. I need food before I finish the rest of my tasks for the day, and all I know how to cook is breakfast.

As the bacon sizzles, I consider looking for a sugar daddy. There has to be an app for that, right? I laugh at the thought. But at least then, I could buy the property next door, fully fund my bed-and-breakfast, and maybe have sex. Doesn't seem like such a bad gig. As long as my sugar daddy is hot and not three times my age.

I go onto the dating app and playfully update my profile, knowing it will probably be a mistake.

Summer Jones. Twenty-nine. Female. Future business owner. Horse lover. Searching for a sugar daddy.

At least now, maybe the *rich* weirdos will come out of hiding.

2

BECKETT

I lead two mares into the center of the barn and set pads and saddles on their backs. After I cinch the leather strap, I make sure it's tight around the belly. Just as I'm walking around Lollipop, I see my younger brother Harrison walking up with a big white to-go cup, which I know came from the deli and is full of tea.

"You're tellin' me you went to town to grab lunch and didn't even offer to grab me anything?"

He shrugs. "You're a big boy."

"Bastard." I say it under my breath as I slip the bit into the horse's mouth and put the leather of the bridle behind her ears. "You probably met Gracie for lunch, didn't you?"

Grace is his best friend, who I swear he has a crush on, though he will never admit it.

"Yeah, actually, I did."

"You propose yet?"

He rolls his eyes. "For the five-hundredth time, we're just friends. Never even fucked before."

"Right. Like *anyone* believes that. So you're joinin' the lesson today?" I give him a shocked look, then walk over to Popsicle and put on her bridle.

"You think I'm here for my health?" He chugs his drink, making a sound like it's the most refreshing beverage he's ever had. I consider snatching it from his hands and gulping it down to teach him a lesson.

"No pranks today." I hope he'll get the hint from my stern voice. My gut tells me he won't, probably because he never does. Harrison always has some kind of joke up his sleeve and never passes up an opportunity to make someone laugh, even at his own expense. He's five years younger than me, but damn, with the amount of energy he has combined with his unwavering commitment to being a total asshole, he makes me feel like I'm ancient. However, he's as charming as a prince when it comes to pretty women.

"No pranks," he repeats, leading Tinker Bell and Peter Pan —two chestnut-brown quarter horses with black manes—from the back stalls so he can saddle them up for us. The two horses are siblings, and we bought and trained them six years ago. "Whatever you say, boss."

We teach riding lessons out of my parents' bright green barn on the Bar V Ranch, and people of all ages drive from surrounding areas to our stables. We have some of the best trails in Texas right in our backyard, landscaped by trees and mountains. After some city-girl influencer made a video about our services, we've been booked nonstop by women searching for their own personal cowboy man candy.

The number of phone numbers I've gotten could fill a phone book if those things still existed around here.

At this point, Harrison and I are a package deal, and many of the women who've booked our services have requested we both be available. It's a good cop, bad cop situation, but I'm still not sure which one he is because the rules never apply to him.

"Who're our clients today?"

I tug on the saddle horns, making sure they're tight enough. "We've got Pamela and Patricia. They're sisters."

"Mm. Twins?" His brow perks up.

"No. And you're keeping your dick in your pants. No more sleepin' with the clients."

He laughs. "You don't own my dick, big bro."

"I'll tell Dad."

"Is that supposed to be a threat?" He walks into the tack room and grabs a saddle bag, and I'm almost tempted to search it before he attaches the pack to his horse. Make sure there aren't any rubber rats or plastic spiders this time.

"Not a threat, little brother. A goddamn promise. Ya know Dad would flip his shit if he knew half the crap you pulled."

"You're so uptight. Ya gotta live a little. Go have a one-night stand or somethin'. Otherwise, your balls are gonna shrivel up like raisins."

I glare at him. "You're insufferable."

"I'm not the one who backs into parking spots. That's you. Total douchebag."

Before I can open my mouth to say anything, a noise behind me interrupts us.

"Hi!" I hear over my shoulder and put on my million-dollar smile for our clients. They're sisters, around my mawmaw's age. I glance over at my annoying sidekick. "This is my younger brother Harri—"

"Harrison!" Patricia gleams. "We saw you online. You're just too a-dor-a-ble. Might want to put you in my purse and bring you home to my granddaughter."

"Granddaughter, you say. Got a pic?"

I clear my throat, keeping my cool but still putting on the Southern charm for the city dwellers.

She pulls out her phone and flips through her pics, landing on it.

"Beauuuuuuuuuutiful. How old is she?" He's stressing his drawl.

I grab Lollipop's and Popcicle's lead ropes as they make small talk, and by some miracle, Harrison decides to help. He gleefully leads the training horses and the women outside as I finish saddling our mares.

They're so enamored by him, laughter echoes throughout the barn. I doubt they'll notice I'm not around, but I make quick work of saddling up. I lead our horses outside, then tie the reins to a watering post.

Harrison is still going on about Patricia's granddaughter. "Maybe you should've brought her with ya." He winks at Pamela, who blushes. I'm pretty sure, at this point, they want him for themselves.

"Howdy." I smile. "Y'all almost ready to get goin'?"

Harrison explains the dos and don'ts, and all the need-to-knows of the saddle. They listen to him intently. It's probably the only time he takes this job seriously. No one has ever gotten injured on our watch, and we'd like to keep it that way.

"You're not gonna let this horse run away with me, right?" Pamela turns to me.

"No, ma'am. They're gentle creatures. They don't spook or nothin'. We put three-year-olds on Lollipop and Popsicle." Her shoulders slightly relax. "You're in good hands."

"Strong hands?" Patricia bats her eyelashes, and a smile forms on her lips.

"Yes, ma'am. The strongest." Harrison pats her on the back.

We teach riding lessons because we're passionate about riding. It's not for the money. When people leave Bar V, we want them to talk about their experience, so it's important to me that they have a good time and not be scared.

"I ain't gonna let nothin' happen to ya." Harrison beams at them. "Now, you can get up the old-fashioned way by usin' the stirrup, or I can get the stepladder for ya." He points over at it.

"Oh, with my weary bones, you might as well give me the easy way. I don't think I have the strength." Pamela places her hand on her hip.

Harrison shoots her a wink and grabs the ladder.

"Which horse ya want?" I look at Patricia.

"Lollipop," she immediately says, and Pamela laughs.

"Now remember, this ain't Disney World. These are real animals in a real environment. But I can tell you that we've never had an incident for as long as we've been teachin' lessons, which for me is two decades."

They both laugh. "Twenty years? When did ya start, in the womb?"

I grin. "When I was twelve."

"Hopefully, we won't break your record."

"Nah, there's no way," I proudly say as Harrison returns with the ladder. We help the ladies climb up, and they lift their legs over the saddle and position themselves. Harrison explains the stirrups and the reins again and ensures we'll be beside them if anything gets weird. Once they're situated, we hop on our horses and lead them down the Pondview Trail. It's my absolute favorite.

The sun is high in the sky, and there's a light breeze. It's a great day for a ride.

"How sore am I going to be tomorrow?" Patricia asks.

"*Very*." Harrison glances at her over his shoulder with a smirk.

I shake my head with a laugh as we continue forward.

Eventually, the trail narrows, and I can see the clearing in the distance. This is one of my favorite places in the world. It's special to me, and when I was in high school, I used to throw pond parties out here.

My younger siblings still do sometimes, and there's a firepit that's used during the cowboy trail rides in the summer. We pitch tents for guests, cook chili and beans on the fire, and play guitar. It's an homage to the culture deeply ingrained in me, and everyone in my family, although not all of us work on the ranch.

Pamela chuckles to herself. "Horseback riding has been a bucket list item of mine."

"Yeah?"

She nods. "Growing up in Houston, it's not always so easy to do real Texan things like this."

"Glad y'all joined us then and let us pop your horseback riding cherry." Harrison smirks.

I glare at him and then back at them. "Apologies for his antics."

They laugh, loving it, and I'm glad because Harrison has a way of saying things he shouldn't at the most inappropriate times.

When we make it to the clearing, I lead the way to the tying posts by the pond's bank. We help the ladies off the horses and allow them to stretch.

"Only problem with getting off is…ya gotta get back on." Harrison snickers. The innuendos are relentless. "But I gotcha covered."

They walk around, picking yellow wildflowers. We take pictures of them with the horses and together. It's a photo op.

When I turn my back, I hear Patricia yell at the top of her lungs. "Snake!" she screams, pointing.

Harrison has it tied to a fishing line and is tugging at it. I make my way over toward them.

Pamela is laughing so hard, she's squeezing her legs together. "I'm gonna piss myself. Too funny." She was obviously in on the joke, because she has her cell phone out recording.

"Are you going to share this online?" Patricia looks horrified.

"Yes, I am!" she chokes out, unable to breathe because she finds it so funny. "You're going viral."

"I'm so sorry. Are you okay?" I walk over to Patricia, who's swatting her golden-blond hair away from her face.

"Now you're gonna have to message my granddaughter for that. You owe me one! Probably took a year off my life!" She grins at Harrison.

Harrison chuckles. "I'm sorry, Mrs. Patricia." He drops to

one knee and plucks a few flowers from the ground, then offers them to her. "Will you forgive me?"

She takes his gift and grabs his cheek like he's a kid. "I guess. But only because you're cute."

I shake my head. "If you want me to kick his ass after y'all leave, I'll be obliged, ma'am."

"It's fine. But I do have a question for you. Are ya married?" She meets my eyes.

"Nah." I remove my cowboy hat and swipe my hair back.

"Why not?"

I chuckle. "Now you're soundin' like my mama. Just haven't found the right girl yet."

Harrison laughs. "Tell them the truth."

Of course, they perk up.

"Tell us!" Pamela and Patricia are intrigued.

"I don't know what he's talking about." I glare at him.

"He's got a crush on our sister's best friend. Always has." Harrison gives me a smug look.

"I absolutely do not. We *despise* each other. Always have."

The ladies grin. "How long have you crushed on her?"

I could punch Harrison in the gut for this, but instead, I force a smile. "He's got jokes, ma'am. Trust me, it would *never* work out between us."

"That's what they always say." Pamela shakes her head.

"I've been beggin' him to grow some huevos and tell Summer how he feels, but he won't."

I ball my hand into a fist. "I don't have a *thang* for her."

"You do. That's so cute." Patricia waggles her brows.

I'm so aggravated as Harrison bursts into laughter. This has been an ongoing joke with everyone in the family since high school. Summer and I can't even hold a civil conversation without it ending with us at each other's throats.

I brush it off and shrug. "Y'all want to take some pics in the saddle?"

Thankfully, the subject is changed. I'm handed their fancy

smartphones with several lenses on the back. We line the horses up by a few benches that look out at the water and help them climb into the saddles. Harrison holds the horses by the halter and poses. I snap several pictures, and then it's time for us to go.

"Yeehaw," Harrison hoots, walking to his horse, then we slowly make our way back to the barn.

Patricia and Pamela are all smiles when their feet are back on the ground. Their cheeks and noses are sunburned from being out without a hat. They ask for a selfie, and we take a few, then give them hugs goodbye.

"Hope to see y'all again!" I wave as they climb into their car.

They're giddy and happy, and that's the only way I like to see our customers leave. When they're out of sight, I turn to Harrison with a death glare.

"The rubber snake?" I meet his eyes with disdain.

He's smirking. "You know for a fact they fuckin' loved it."

"You nearly gave her a heart attack!"

He shrugs. "But I didn't. That's all that matters. And I'll be messaging her dirty little granddaughter, too, a promise I made."

"You'll never learn," I tell him as he removes the saddles and pads from the training horses, and I take care of ours. "Oh, thanks for mentioning Summer, asshole." I carry two of the saddles by the horns and take them to the tack room.

"Do somethin' about it."

"For the thousandth time, y'all need to stop saying that bullshit and telling people. Ya know how rumors around here spread."

He chuckles. "Everyone already knows, ya dummy."

"I often wonder why I got paired to work with you. None of our other siblings are quite as annoying."

He bursts into laughter. "It's 'cause the rest of them don't want to deal with your grumpy ass."

"Whatever. But hey, I owe you one. I'm totally gonna get you back. It might not be tomorrow. It might not be next week. Hell, it could be years from now, but I will take the perfect opportunity to return the favor and embarrass the living fuck outta ya. Just wait."

"Oooh, I'm shakin' in my boots right now." He wobbles his knees, pretending to be scared, but I know he's not even threatened. Harrison is immune.

I watch him for a few more seconds. "Keep it up, bud. I don't get back. I get even."

"I look forward to it. Sticks and stones and all that jazz."

After we finish cleaning up for the day, Harrison and I muck the stalls and feed the horses. Together, we make fast work of it, and I'm surprised we're finished by five.

"Where're ya headin'?" Harrison pulls his keys from his pocket.

"Gonna go to the grocery store. Ya need anything? I probably shouldn't even ask you, considerin' you didn't grab me a burger today."

He snickers. "Nah, I'm good. Same time tomorrow?"

"Yeah."

I make my way to town.

There is a lot of traffic on the streets, and I realize how much of a disaster it was coming at this time. I drive around the building and find zero parking, so I use a side street and walk a short distance. While my fridge is somewhat bare, I'm only grabbing a few things for tonight, so I hope it won't take long.

As I look at the ribeyes, Mrs. Jacobson, a recently widowed woman, who I'm sure murdered her husband, moves in beside me. She's so close, I can smell her perfume and the mintiness of the gum she's chewing. She's in her early forties but still hasn't learned manners about personal space.

"Hi, Beck." She shortens my name, something only my friends do.

I'm polite and smile, but I'm not in the mood. "Hi, Mrs. Jacobson."

"I've told you time and again, call me Tracie."

I move my attention back to the steaks.

"Those jeans are lookin' mighty fine on you today." Her eyes trail me from head to toe, purposely checking out my ass. This isn't anything new. Plenty of women around town want to become an etch on my headboard, and when I was in my twenties, I wasn't afraid to fuck and forget them. But things are different now.

"I want you to teach me a lesson," she hums.

I meet her eyes, not taking the bait.

"A riding lesson."

A grin touches my lips, but it's forced. The last thing I want is for her to contact my mama and say I was rude in public. "With all due respect, Mrs. Jacobson—"

"Tracie." She bats her fake eyelashes at me.

"Right. We're booked until the end of the year." I pull a business card from my wallet and hand it to her. "Go to the site and sign up. I'd be happy to get ya on the schedule."

She takes it and looks it over. "Just the office number is listed."

"Yes, ma'am." I find a fat steak and grin. "Nice seein' ya again."

I make my way to the freezer section and grab a pint of ice cream, then remind myself to pick some zucchini from the garden when I get home. Right now, though, all I want to do is get the hell out of here.

The long line means it takes nearly thirty minutes for me to check out. By the time I make it to my truck, the sun is setting. On the way home, I cruise with the windows down, feeling the warmth of the early May breeze, enjoying the season change and all the excitement around town. The Fourth of July celebration, the summer festival, and everything we do to bring in visitors are highlights for me.

I pass the Lazy J Ranch, and I see a blonde outside nailing a sign to a post at the Horseshoe Creek Ranch. Taking my foot off the gas, I slow down. At the last minute, I decide to pull over. I don't mind being a nosy neighbor, considering my family's ranch is on the other side.

I get out of the truck and make my way over to her.

"Howdy, ma'am." I give her a smile.

"Hi." She shows her pearly white teeth and perfect smile, making sure to look me up and down. She's attractive and flirty, a deadly combination.

"I'm Beckett Valentine. I live right next door at the Bar V Ranch. What's goin' on?" I glance at the big for sale sign she's struggling to hammer into the wood. "Need some help?"

"Do you mind?" She happily hands everything to me, and I make quick work of it. "For sale, huh?"

"Yeah, my grandparents own the place, and they've decided to sell so they can move to Florida and be closer to all the grandchildren."

"Ahh." I hand the hammer back to her. "How much they askin'?"

"Oh, they've decided to make it a closed bidding process for locals since the place has been in the family for so long. Grandpa said he couldn't stand selling it to some city slicker—his words, not mine—who was out to make some bucks. Are you *interested*?" Her gaze trails down my body again.

I smirk. "I might be."

"All reasonable bids will be considered, and I get to make the final say."

"Really? Well then. Sorry, sweetheart, I didn't get your name."

She instantly blushes. "Natalie."

"Natalie. You busy tomorrow night?"

She grins. "Not yet."

"Ya like Mexican food?"

"Love it. Let me give you my number."

Natalie pulls her phone from her pocket and hands it to me. I put my number into her contacts, then hand it back.

"Join me for dinner tomorrow. I'll pick ya up. I mean, unless you got a boyfriend, fiancé, or husband back home."

"Single as can be." She bites the corner of her lip.

"Great. It's a date, then. Text me?"

My phone immediately buzzes.

"I gotcha saved. Nice meetin' ya, Natalie. Lookin' forward to tomorrow."

"Nice meeting you as well."

I give her a wink before climbing back into my truck, not believing the Horseshoe Creek Ranch is for sale.

As I drive home, I think about the training facility I could build next door and the extra trails I could add to my lessons. The possibilities run wild in my mind. Purchasing land wasn't something I planned to do just yet, but now that the opportunity has presented itself, I can't pass it up.

The Horseshoe Creek will be mine come hell or high water.

3

SUMMER

I grab my to-go mug of coffee and when walking down the steps of my porch, I notice the rosemary I planted beside my steps is dead. It's so dead it looks crispy like someone fried it.

I swear, it didn't look like this yesterday, or maybe it did. Now, I don't remember. I try to think back to the last time I watered it. Peeking to the other side of the steps, I realize my other one looks the same. It doesn't matter if they're in pots or in the ground, they all have the same fate.

"Well, shit." I grab the potted plants Kinsley talked shit about yesterday and move them to the side of the house where all the other plant carcasses live. At least fifteen dried soil pots sit there with sticks poking out of them.

The nursery in town used to have a policy that if a plant died within thirty days, it could be returned. Then I started shopping there, and that ended after my tenth exchange. At this rate, it's so bad I don't think I could keep a cactus alive. It's not like I want one anyway. It's late spring, and I want colorful tulips and mountain laurels.

Give me any plant, and I bet it will be a goner by the end of the week. I've wished for a green thumb, even asked Kinsley to manifest one for me, but somehow I've still got the touch of death.

Dang it. Maybe one day that will change, but it's definitely not today.

I climb inside my Jeep and take the drive across the property to my parents' house. Mom offered to make breakfast this morning, and I had some business to discuss, so I agreed to wake up early and meet them.

As soon as I walk in, Mom greets me with a smile and places a huge plate of pancakes in the center of the table. Strawberry and maple syrup are already out, and a slab of butter. My stomach immediately growls.

"Mornin', sweetie." She swipes loose hairs away from her face with the back of her hand.

"Good mornin', Mama."

Dad comes down the stairs holding a coffee mug and smelling like Old Spice and toothpaste. I'll associate those two scents with him for the rest of my life.

"Mornin', Daddy." I see shaving cream still on one side of his cheek. "Missed a spot." I reach forward, swiping it away, then wipe it on my leg. Looks like he just cleaned up his mustache.

"Thank ya." He moves to the coffee pot and refills his mug.

I turn to Mom. "Need any help?"

"Sure." She nods.

I grab the plates with sausage patties and scrambled eggs. There are also biscuits and cream gravy that have sausage bits in it. My mouth waters with anticipation. I can't remember the last time I had a cowboy breakfast. I've been sticking with omelets lately.

"What's the occasion?" I pile food onto my plate.

"You tell us." Dad grins wide.

"Well…" I grow nervous, something I didn't anticipate. "Did you hear the Horseshoe Creek Ranch is goin' up for sale?"

Dad's face contorts as Mom shakes her head. "Everything okay with the Whitleys?"

"Oh yeah, they're fine. Just want to move to Florida to be closer to their family," I explain.

"That's understandable. I think they have sixteen grandkids or somethin' now. I saw Mary Lee at the gas station the other day."

I don't waste any time and rip the Band-Aid off. "I want to buy it."

Dad's eyebrow pops up as Mom watches me.

"But I know I won't have enough savings to cover it, so I'm asking for help. I'm gonna go to the bank and get a loan, but I thought maybe you could let me borrow some money for the down payment. Of course, I'll pay back every single penny, with a little interest."

Mom and Dad hold a silent conversation with each other, something they've done for as long as I can remember.

"How much?" Dad places squares of butter between each pancake in his stack.

"Not sure. They're doing a bidding thing for locals. The highest reasonable bid wins."

Mom swallows a bite of sausage. "So you don't know what the starting bid is?"

I shake my head. "No. But I did some research last night and checked how much that cattle ranch up in the mountains sold for a few years ago."

Dad doesn't hesitate. "Five million."

I glance over at him. "Well, I shoulda just called and asked if you knew."

He chuckles. "I bet next door is worth about that. The property isn't as large as ours or the Valentine's. I think it's close to a thousand acres, but it does have that natural creek and some nice landscaping. Plus the old Whitley home. I think it's ten bedrooms or somethin' like that. Used to play inside it as a kid."

Thinking about Dad as a young boy running through that old farmhouse makes me smile.

"Perfect place for that bed-and-breakfast you've been dreamin' about since you were old enough to make a waffle." Mom winks.

"I know. But I also know it's a lot of money. I think I can make it profitable within five years. You know how many tourists come into town for the Fourth of July and how many bikers swing through going up to Big Bend. The inn above the general store only has a few rooms, and it's booked up until New Year's. I even heard they have a waitlist for cancellations. I did market research and some math." I pull my phone from my pocket. "Eight of ten rooms, booked 365 nights a year for $200 a night, will put me at around $700,000 a year after expenses. I could have it fully paid off within five years with some advertising. Kinsley even told me she'd help, and you know she's a pro at that stuff."

Mom and Dad hold another silent conversation. They know this has been my dream ever since I was a kid, and I'm serious about it.

"And who will do the renovations for the house?" Dad glances at me.

"I'm not sure yet, but Colt Valentine is a handyman, and I think I could get the family discount. Plus, I could always bribe him with free room and board for *guests*."

He chuckles. "Have you gone down to the bank yet?"

"No. But my credit is perfect. I checked my savings, and I have a little over a hundred and fifty thousand in there now." Since I was eighteen, my parents have given me a salary to help manage the horses and assist with cattle trading. Living on the ranch means I barely have any bills, so I've been saving and splurging on plants.

"With a loan, you'll need to put down fifteen percent. That's a lot of money, sweetie. You know we don't like buyin' things on credit."

"I know, but the opportunity is too good to pass up."

"I agree. Get a preapproval from the bank first and we'll go from there…"

My heart is racing, and I'm so giddy with excitement I stop eating.

Dad clears his throat. "I only hope no one else is lookin' to buy it. Otherwise, it could become a lot more expensive."

"I know. I've asked around, and so far, I'm the only one interested. They'll close the bidding in three weeks. I'm going to start at a low but reasonable offer. Maybe I'll get a deal."

"Good luck, sweetie." Dad grins.

I rush over and wrap my arm around his neck.

"Thank you." I'm nearly in tears when I move to Mom to give her a hug, too. "Thank you so much. I won't let you down."

"I know you won't." Dad picks up his mug and takes a sip of coffee.

I'm buzzing with so much energy, I finish my breakfast and start cleaning the kitchen with a pep in my step. I give Dad another hug before he leaves to take care of ranch business, then I help Mom clean the kitchen.

"Proud of you, honey. You know, considerin' you're our only kid, we'd hang the moon for you."

"I know, Mama. I'm so grateful."

She smiles sweetly. "You know you gotta make Grandma's secret chocolate chip cookie recipe for the guests."

"That's an incredible idea!" Right now, so many things are running through my mind. I open my phone and make a B&B wish list so I don't forget.

"You know we want to see ya succeed, Summer. We're always here for you."

I smile wide. "I don't know what I did in my past life to deserve y'all as parents."

Mom chuckles, wiping her hands on a dishrag. "Yeah, yeah. Now, go make us proud."

"I will!" I give her another hug, then leave. A nervous excitement swarms through me as I take the winding road that leads straight to the bank. They're busy today, but I find a parking spot right in front—a good omen.

The dark red-bricked building is one of the first built in Valentine, Texas. A historical marker even says as much by the front entrance.

When I enter, I'm greeted by name because everyone around here knows everyone. I sit in a chair by the windows while I wait to speak to the loan officer. My palms are sweaty, and I don't know why I'm so dang nervous. Maybe it's because I'm so close to getting what I've always wanted.

Good things don't typically happen to me, so I'm trying not to get my hopes up too high.

"Summer Jones," Mrs. McAdams says from the corner office. Her daughter used to babysit me after school when my parents were caught up with the ranch.

"It's been so long. How have you been, honey?" She's well put together, wearing high heels that are more like stilts, so she stands taller than me.

"Fantastic." I give her a smile, taking a seat in the chair across from her desk. Her office is welcoming and smells like cinnamon and vanilla, and the tension in my body slowly melts away.

"So what brings you in today?"

"I wanted to apply for a loan."

"Oh really?" She almost seems shocked.

It *is* shocking.

"Yeah, did you hear the Horseshoe Creek Ranch is for sale?"

"That's interesting. I haven't been told that one yet."

A part of me wishes I would've kept it to myself. However, I know it won't be long until the entire town knows. The more people who know means the more competition I could potentially have. I give her a few more details, and she slides an application across the desk, along with a black ballpoint pen. The ink dances across the paper as I fill out the form. It's an old-school way of doing things, but that's just how things go in Valentine.

Once it's complete, she scans and emails it to the manager, whose office is right next door.

"It might take some time to get this approved. Do you have a cosigner?"

The word feels heavy. "No, I didn't think about that."

"With a purchase that's over seven figures, you'd need something to ensure the bank would be paid for their investment if something happened. You don't have a lengthy credit history."

"I understand. I'll have to figure something out."

"Also, you'll want to put at least fifteen percent down. Twenty is better."

I ask a few more questions about the preapproval process and how it works, and she explains everything to me in great detail. By the time I'm finished chatting about numbers, approvals, and everything else, my brain is like mashed potatoes.

"Anything else?" Mrs. McAdams's kind eyes meet mine.

"No, I think that's it." I stand, giving her a handshake.

"Oh honey, don't forget to take a sucker." She holds her hand out, presenting the bowl of Dum-Dums. I chuckle, reaching forward and grabbing a mystery flavor one. This was a tradition when I was little, and I'm glad she hasn't forgotten.

"Guess I've been good today." I unwrap the paper and pop the brown sucker into my mouth. "Do you know what flavor mystery is?"

She shakes her head.

"The factory doesn't either. They pour whatever flavoring is left at the end of the day into the mold and wah-lah…you have mystery flavor."

"Is that true?" She tilts her head.

I shrug. "I don't know. A friend told me that, but I believe her. They never quite taste the same."

When I walk outside, the sun seems to be shining brighter, the birds are chirping louder, and I have this feeling deep inside that the ranch is going to be mine. Maybe this is the woo that Kinsley is always talking about, but I like the way it feels.

Since she's on my mind, I send her a few texts, giving her a rundown of everything that's transpired since I woke up. She immediately calls me.

"Oh my God! It's going to be yours! I swear. I just have this gut feeling that it's going to happen!"

I squeal as I get into my Jeep. "Everything seems to be falling into place. I have a few loose ends to tie up for the preapproval, then I hope to make the offer by the time they post the listing. I'm crossing my fingers!"

"I'm crossing my damn toes!" Kinsley giggles. "What're you doin' tonight?"

"Last I checked, nothing."

"Perfect! Let's do dinner. I know it's barely lunchtime, but ya girl already needs some ninety-nine cent margaritas. Plus, we have to celebrate."

"There's not anything to celebrate yet."

"Uh, yeah, there is. We're treating it like it already happened. It's called manifesting, baby! Just keep believing it's yours and it is. No doubts."

I shake my head but laugh. "Okay, okay. What time?"

"Seven."

"I'll be there!" My excitement quickly rebuilds, then we hang up.

This is happening.

The Horseshoe Creek has my name written all over it.

I'm officially turning woo.

4

BECKETT

*T*he hot water falls over my sore muscles, and I allow the stream to pound against my skin. While I train people to ride horses, I also train horses for people to ride. It goes full circle in my world.

The alarm I set—so I wouldn't spend too much time in the shower—buzzes. Tonight, I have a date with Natalie, and considering I want to schmooze her into selling me the Horseshoe Creek Ranch, the impression has to be top-notch.

I *always* get what I want, and I'm not afraid to flirt if that's what it takes. After I slide on a black T-shirt and some jeans, I put on my boots and grab a baseball hat. Then I head to Rancho Grande, where she said she'd meet me. I'm relieved because I sometimes find the getting-to-know-you conversations before a date awkward.

As soon as I enter the restaurant, I immediately smell the meaty scents of sizzling fajitas. I spot Natalie on the patio outside, typing away on her phone. The weather is perfect, it's not too hot or warm, and the twinkle lights strung above the covered area set the mood.

"Hi." I pull out the chair and sit in front of her.

She drinks me in, smiling. "Hello. Was almost afraid you weren't going to show."

I smirk. "I never miss a date with a pretty lady."

Instantly, she blushes.

People chatting, plates and silverware clanking, and music from overhead. Before I can say anything else, the server walks over.

"I'll take a margarita with salt."

Natalie orders the same.

When we're alone again, I meet her eyes.

"So tell me about yourself." I genuinely want to learn more about her.

"I'm thirty-two."

"Me too."

She chuckles. "Just broke up with my fiancé of five years before getting on a plane and coming here."

When our margaritas are delivered, we quickly give our food order and continue the conversation.

"May I ask why?"

She stirs the straw in her mug a few times, then takes a big drink. "I was bored."

This makes me laugh. "Bored?"

"Yeah. I'm not getting any younger, and I'm tired of"—her voice lowers to a near whisper—"missionary."

"Ahh. Yeah, I understand that. But did you love him?"

"Of course. I just can't imagine forever with him. Loving someone and being in love with them are two totally different things. So I thought I'd visit Valentine for a month and meet someone willing to show me a good time."

I grin. "How's that working out for you?"

"I'm here with you, aren't I?"

"Touché." Natalie's a nice girl, pretty, but she seems like she's looking for a random hookup, something I'm not necessarily wanting. However, never say never. "Here's a question for ya. Would you ever consider moving here?"

Her face contorts. "No way. I need the beach and to feel the sand between my toes as badly as I need air. I mean, don't get me wrong, Valentine is great. But it's no Miami."

"You're right about that."

"What about you? Would you ever leave this place?"

I shake my head. "Nah. Sometimes a person is destined to live a slower-paced life where things are easy. It's home. Not sure I could ever leave Valentine. My quadruple great-grandfather founded this town."

"Oh! The last name, duh. Totally makes sense now. Should've put two and two together."

I laugh, and as I'm opening my mouth to say something else, in walks my sister Kinsley and the woman who has somehow burrowed herself under my skin for the past fifteen years—Summer Jones.

"Well, shit," I mutter, knowing I'll never be able to avoid them.

Natalie turns around and makes eye contact with my sister, then looks back at me. "Your girlfriend?"

"No, my little sister and her rude-as-hell best friend."

Natalie laughs. "I know exactly how that is. Trust me."

Moments later, Kinsley and Summer are being sat two tables over from us. It doesn't take long for my sister to spot me, and she makes her way over.

"Howdy!" She turns to Natalie. "I'm Kinsley, Beck's *favorite* sister."

I nearly choke on my drink. "Nah. Vera is much nicer than you."

"She's sixteen."

"And?"

Kinsley shakes her head, then looks at my date.

"I'm Natalie Whitley."

"Oh yeah. I think I spoke to you on the phone about the Horseshoe Creek Ranch."

"Kinsley Valentine. Yes, I remember." Natalie looks like she's recalling the conversation.

"So are you two on a date or somethin'?" Kinsley's question comes out ruder than I think she intended.

"Yeah. So can you please go away?" I glance over at Summer, who groans, then holds up the menu, blocking me from seeing her reaction. The woman always orders the same thing and has since we were teenagers, so I know she's not reading a word. I'd bet my ass she orders tamales with chili con queso and double refried beans. To anyone else, she's deciding, but I know better. I know *her.* And she's pissed.

"Have you gotten any offers yet? I saw the sign in front of the main driveway yesterday when I drove home." Kinsley uses her sugary-sweet tone. It's amazing how quickly she can flick the charm off and on.

"I'm buying the ranch." I don't hesitate when I say it.

Natalie chuckles. "*Cocky.* I love that."

I give her a wink. "It's mine. We both know it."

Kinsley's mouth falls open, and I hear Summer slam the menu onto the table. Seems everyone is shocked about this announcement except for Natalie, who's grinning wide.

"What do you mean you're buying the ranch?" Kinsley's brow furrows. "This is a joke, right?"

"Did I stutter?"

She glares at me.

"I want it. It's right next door to Mom and Dad's, the perfect location for me and Harrison to expand our training facility. What's the big deal?"

"You can't afford that." Kinsley doesn't believe me.

"Sis, you have no idea how much money I have." I reach forward, placing my hand on top of Natalie's, who picks up her margarita, clearly enjoying the show. "Tell them."

Natalie shrugs, sitting up a little straighter. "As of now, you have the winning bid. Would love to sell it to you."

Kinsley huffs. "I did not have this on my BINGO card."

"Well, sis, sorry. Maybe if you came around every once in a while, you'd have known I'd already put an offer in earlier today."

"A very generous one at that. Wouldn't be surprised if you do get it in the end." Natalie is confident about me winning. The odds are totally in my favor.

"Me neither." I pull my hand away as the server returns, and we order another round of drinks.

Kinsley awkwardly stands to the side and waits.

When the server walks off, she clears her throat. "Do Mom and Dad know about this?"

"No one knows but Natalie, you, me"—I glance over at Summer—"and your nosy-ass bestie sitting over there listening to our conversation with her supersonic hearing."

Summer rolls her eyes.

"Okay then, well. Enjoy your *date*, I *guess*." Kinsley gives me a sarcastic smile and then returns to their table.

Natalie and I continue our conversation, but from my periphery, I can see Summer nearly exploding with anger. She's big mad, and it takes every ounce of control I have not to burst into laughter.

No telling what crawled up her ass and died today, but then again, she always acts this way when we're in the same room.

5

SUMMER

$\mathcal{K}$ insley returns to the table and plops down in front of me with a confused look on her face.

"I ordered us extra tequila shots with our margaritas." I need something to calm me down because I hate that I can hear every damn word Beckett says to Natalie.

"Good, I think we're gonna need them. Did you—"

"Overhear? Yes." I meet her brown eyes. "I'm pissed."

"I'm so sorry. I seriously had no idea Beck was interested in that land." She keeps her voice hushed so he can't overhear our conversation. "He's never mentioned *anything* about wanting to expand his business before, so it's coming from left field. I wouldn't have kept that from you."

"I know. It's not your fault. You can't control him. Hell, no one can."

She chuckles. "Yeah. You're right about that. I just hate how competitive he is."

"I'm unhappy. I'm also very aware he has the money after that woman posted that video of him and Harrison."

"They are booked until the end of the year. Ugh," Kinsley groans when Natalie laughs.

As soon as our tequila shots are set onto the table, we pick

36

them up, lick the salt off the rim, and shoot them back. We bite into our limes, and right now, I just want it to take my anger away. Tough luck, though. It doesn't even take the edge off.

Chips and salsa are set in front of us, and Kinsley and I place our orders and then dig in. I get the same thing I always do.

When Beckett chuckles, I glance over at him. Our eyes meet, a silent conversation passes between us, and when my cheeks heat, I bring my gaze to Kinsley. I hate that even after all these years, he still has the ability to affect me from all the way across the damn room.

"Listen, it's gonna all work out for the absolute best." Confidence oozes from her.

"I love your positivity, but I'm not convinced." I pick up my margarita and take a drink. I swear it doesn't taste like there's a drop of alcohol in it.

"Remember what I've taught you? Ya gotta be a believer. If it's meant for you, you'll have it."

"Sometimes, you're just a little too woo. I can't make money magically appear, Kins. And you know if it grew on trees, I'd kill it." I let out a sigh.

"Look, I'll find out all the details I can. I know it's my brother and all, but I'm rooting for *you*. He doesn't need the property. He can continue doing what he's doing on my parents' land."

"Yeah, but we both know how he gets. When he wants something, he doesn't back down. Beckett is fuckin' relentless." I growl. "I *hate* him."

"Right now, I kinda hate him, too." She snickers. Kinsley loves her brother and every person in her family. If asked, she'd do anything for him, as long as it didn't hurt anyone.

"I wish I couldn't hear what the hell they're saying now." A tinge of jealousy darts through me as Beckett leans closer to Natalie.

"Right. He's not *that* funny. Too much of a grump. Pretty sure she just wants to fuck him like everyone else does."

"Not *everyone*."

She lifts a brow.

I lean forward and lower my voice. "I don't!"

"Girl, you're two tequila shots away from rollin' around in the sheets with him."

"Bullshit!" The word falls loudly out of my mouth. Beckett glances my way and glares at Kinsley. "He was definitely put on this earth to drive me absolutely crazy!"

I hate how smooth and flirty he is.

"You hated him in high school, but still? It's been fifteen years. At this point, I'm convinced you're madly in love with each other." She sips her margarita.

"Hell no."

"What's the saying? Denial isn't just a river in Egypt."

I throw a chip at her, and she slaps it away. "Trust me, if the entire human race depended on the two of us getting together, I'd let it go extinct."

She looks at me incredulously. "Come on. Lie to someone else."

"Lie? Okay, well, I can admit he's good-lookin', and maybe I *would* bang him. *If*...I could duct tape his mouth closed."

Kinsley snickers. "See, that wasn't too hard to admit, was it? Now all you have to do is marry him."

"Eww, no. That would be a lifetime of torture. Ugh."

Natalie's encouraging him way too much. She's literally putty in his big, strong, calloused hands. When she laughs, I roll my eyes.

After two margaritas and two shots of tequila, our food is delivered. My stomach growls when I dip chips into my beans. I take a bite of one of my tamales and try to focus on my food and Kinsley. With every ounce of strength I have, I try very hard not to pay them any attention, but it's impossible when they're sitting just a few tables away.

"So how's work goin'?"

Kinsley could talk about this for the rest of the night, and I desperately need a change of subject.

"Terrible. I suggested creating an 'Ask Me' column, and Mr. Anderson lost it. I tried to explain it might encourage locals to read more articles, maybe renew their print subscriptions, and it would be fun. Basically, I was told to write my articles and be happy I have a job. I wanted to knee him in the junk."

"Wow, that *would* be an amazing addition to the paper, but you know how he gets. You suggest things, he bats them down, and then as soon as it's his idea, it will be a go. Just give it some time."

"I'm convinced he just doesn't get it. If we continue this trajectory, we won't have a paper, and he won't have a job either."

"When is he planning on retirin'?" I ask.

"Not sure. Should've retired yesterday! He's a pain in my ass."

I snicker and hear Beckett order another round of drinks. I glance back in his direction. The electric current I've always felt tugs my gaze toward him, and he smirks. Those blue eyes meet mine from under that baseball hat, and I hate how attractive he is without even trying.

"So have you decided what to rename the ranch when it's yours?"

She stops me midthought. "Rename it? No, that hasn't crossed my mind. Might just keep it as it is. Horseshoe Creek Ranch is kinda cute. The branding would be adorable.

"Yeah. Oh, I forgot to tell you. I updated my dating app to say I was lookin' for a sugar daddy."

Kinsley nearly chokes on her food. "No, you didn't."

"I did. Zero prospects, though."

"Girl, what if it works, and some billionaire tries to sweep you off your feet and away from Valentine?"

The thought has me snorting. "I'm not ever leaving. This is

home. But I'm not ashamed to let a billionaire buy my ranch and remodel that house."

"They say when your friends get a rich man, everyone wins." She lifts her hand for a high five, and I slam mine against it.

Kinsley looks at her brother and shakes her head. "I guess he's goin' to flirt his way to the top."

"This is unfair. Maybe he'll change his mind, decide it was a mistake, and give up?"

She pops another chip into her mouth. "Doubt it. You're both too stubborn for your own good. But here's a thought… why don't you buy it together, then split the property into sections? Then you both win."

"Absolutely not. I can't imagine having to look at his stupid face every day for the rest of my life. It would never work out. You and I both know that, Kins. We can barely be in the same room together. It's a miracle I haven't flipped him off yet."

She sighs. "You're right. But you know he's not *all* bad, though. Beckett has heart, even if he's an asshole ninety percent of the time."

I suck in a deep breath, thinking back to when I caught glimpses of a person who had a heart and cared. But those moments only lasted for a brief second. Now, I'm almost convinced he never existed, and all the kindness he showed me was a figment of my imagination. Teenage me crushed on an unrealistic version of Beckett, not this monster of a man who drives me crazy with every damn chance he gets. "Doesn't matter. I still hate him." I scoop beans into my mouth.

"I reckon the odds of a ranch coming up for sale so close to your parents is next to nothin'." She sighs.

"That's why I need to ensure that I beat him. You're gonna have to do recon, Kins. Did he say he made a bid?"

She nods.

"Find out his offer, and I'll go down to the bank so I can outbid him. But you gotta use those reporter skills and, shit, be inconspicuous. If he knows how badly I want that ranch, there's no way in hell he'll ever let me win it."

"That settles it, then."

I meet her eyes. "What?"

"Means you gotta play dirty." A sly smile curls her lips.

"Let the games begin."

"That ranch *is* yours, Summer. Gotta do what ya gotta do."

"You're right. I'm gonna take his ass down, cowboy boots and all."

"That's the spirit, bestie." Kinsley winks, and the defeat I felt earlier slowly melts away.

I will get what's rightfully mine—the Horseshoe Creek Ranch.

6

BECKETT

"*C*ome on, now." I click my tongue on the roof of my mouth. For the past thirty minutes, I've been working with this Arabian horse named Dragon, who has given me nothing but hell today.

Mr. Barton dropped him off early yesterday, and his ground manners were excellent. When I unloaded him from the trailer, I thought he'd be a blessing. However, this horse seems like a curse. Dragon's three years old and has an attitude worse than Summer Jones's. That's saying a lot. He bucks, trying to throw me off his back, but I've been training since I was twelve, so this is nothing for me. I just hang on for the wild ride.

I hold the reins tight as he sidesteps, and I squeeze my thighs to keep my balance. "You'll eventually wear out." I keep my voice calm and my focus steady.

"Hey!" Harrison yells, pulling away my much-needed attention as he strolls over to the corral, whistling. The bucking and sprinting start again, but Harrison doesn't seem to notice or care.

"Worst timing ever, bro." Dragon nearly crushes my leg against the metal pen. He's pissed that I'm still on his back even

42

though he's been saddle trained and should be used to carrying weight.

"What a little bastard." Harrison leans his arms against the railing and watches with amusement.

"Captain Obvious is at it again, I see. You're distracting me! Go away!" With every passing second, Dragon grows more agitated. Unfortunately for him, I'm not going anywhere.

"I wasn't talkin' about the horse." Harrison snickers.

"Leave."

"Nah. We got some business to discuss. Just heard the news that you're thinkin' 'bout buying the Horseshoe Creek Ranch."

I glance at him. "I'm busy right at this very moment."

Dragon bucks again, and this time he farts, causing Harrison to bend over and laugh...*hard*. He's like a tween boy nearly gasping for air. Anything to do with farts or poop, and it's game over.

Once he finally catches his breath, he speaks. "So you already put in an offer?"

"Yeah! I fuckin' did. Can we talk about this in like ten minutes?" Dragon is absolutely relentless, and I don't want him to hurt himself or me.

"Nah, now is good. I got somewhere to be in thirty." He unlocks his phone, and I assume he's checking the time. Or maybe he got a text from a side piece, but most likely, since the sun is still up, it's Grace. I don't care at this point. I just want him to stop distracting me. "Anyway, you want to build the state-of-the-art trainin' facility you've been talkin' about?"

I take my focus off the horse for two seconds, and Dragon twists his lower half around. The next thing I know, I'm flying out of the saddle and dropping onto the ground, stomach first. I lie there for a few seconds and ball my hands into fists out of frustration alone. I'm getting too old to have the wind knocked out of me. I push myself up onto my boots, wiping the dust from my jeans and shirt, then glare at Harrison.

I'm gonna kick his ass.

"Such a basic mistake for an all-star trainer."

"Fuck you." I seethe.

"Attitude. Damn. But since you're free and not so tied up in the saddle, can we talk about this?"

"Five. Minutes." I stand firm, and even set the alarm on my phone, because Harrison doesn't respect my boundaries, especially when it comes to work.

I walk up to Dragon, holding out my hand. He takes a step back with the forward motion I take. There's no trust between us, and he's going to be a feisty one. It might take longer to break him. Dragon has to be calm enough for Mr. Barton's ten-year-old son to ride in six months.

I calmly keep my hand outstretched. "I won't hurt you."

He looks at me like I'm the devil, but eventually, his curiosity gets the best of him. He takes a step forward, then another one, until he's sniffing my hand. I grab the reins, gently speaking as I run my hand down his neck. "I think we're done here for the day. We'll try again tomorrow."

The last thing I want to do is cause unnecessary stress on the animal, because that does no one any good. After I walk Dragon to the barn, I unsaddle and lock him in the far stable. Then I return to the corral, where Harrison impatiently waits.

"You're basically edging me over here, damn."

I give him a look. "Gross."

"So you *are* buyin' it?"

I nod, and he claps his hands together with a wide grin. "Hot damn!"

My face contorts. "Why're you so excited?"

"Because that means we'll get to expand." Harrison treats me like I'm the stupid one here.

"*We?* What if I want to buy it so I don't have to work with your annoyin' ass anymore?" I lift my brows, watching him grow shifty. I'm just giving him a hard time, but he doesn't need to know that yet.

"You wouldn't." He narrows his gaze, waiting for me to

crack.

I let him sit in it for a little while longer, then smile. "You're right. Even though you're a pain in my ass, you're my partner. Not sure I'd want to run this business with anyone else."

"Aw, gettin' all soft on me now after nearly makin' me shit my pants?" Harrison throws a fist pump in the air. "Excited, man. Hope you win it. However, I heard you weren't the only person in town shootin' for it."

My eyes look out into the distance, scanning over the prairies. "I'm sure everyone knows at this point."

"Yeah, Summer is ready to take you down. Talkin' shit all over town. Better be careful. She's scary sometimes." He tells me that like I don't already know this.

"Ain't worried about her. She can put her mouth where her money is, and I can guarantee I have more saved."

He smirks. "I got a place she can put her mouth."

I shake my head, and he continues.

"I just hope you're right. Heard through the grapevine that her parents are gonna be helpin' her. I know ya got money, but you ain't got the Jones's type of money. Kinda brings a whole new meanin' to keepin' up with the Joneses, don't it?"

"Of course, they'll support their only child. Should've known it wouldn't be as easy as pie."

"I'll invest too if ya need me to. I got a lot saved. There is no way you're giving in. Some of the trails on that ranch would be incredible for leisure rides."

A smile touches my lips. "I know. I was thinkin' the same thing. Plus, it's got the perfect location for an indoor training arena. Can even invest in more horses. All I gotta do is make sure I win."

"You down for playin' dirty?" Harrison throws me a mischievous grin.

"I want to, but I'm pretty sure I got Natalie Whitley, the granddaughter who's overseein' all this, in my palm. I just gotta submit the highest number, and it's mine."

"Hell yeah!" Harrison holds up his hand for a high five. I smash mine against his, excited about the possibilities. It's almost better than signing the deed. Almost.

We make small talk about our schedule for tomorrow, then I head back to the barn to spend some quality time with Dragon. I brush him and feed him some alfalfa before letting him out of the stall to roam the pasture until dinner.

As I'm mucking a few stalls, my cell rings, and I grin when I see it's my best friend, Cash. He moved to Houston a couple of years ago after graduating from veterinarian school, but we've kept in touch.

"Hey, man, what's up?"

"Dude, my mama just called and told me you were tryin' to buy the Horseshoe Creek Ranch."

I burst into laughter.

"What?" he questions.

"First Harrison and then you. The rumor mill must be working extra hard if *you* heard."

He chuckles. "You know I don't believe half the shit I'm told, but I had to go straight to the source with that one."

"You didn't believe her?" I lean the shovel against the wall of the stall.

"Honestly? No. Had no idea it was for sale. Hell, I might've bought it." He's joking, but I also hear the seriousness behind his tone.

"Dude, put your bid in."

"Nah, I wouldn't do that to ya."

"Thanks. So how are things goin'?"

He quickly answers. "I hate it here. The traffic. The need to impress everyone at social events. Too much prestige."

"Sounds like a livin' hell. I could never do it. No way."

"It is hell. The money is great. But I don't know how much longer I'm gonna be able to take it."

"Money don't mean shit if you're miserable."

"Ya know how much I hate it when you're right?" he asks.

"A lot. Most do. But then again, it's not easy being right all the time." I check the time, not wanting to rush this conversation but knowing I need to get back to it. However, I'm thankful for the break. I've been at it all day, trying to keep my mind busy after finding out Summer wants the property too.

"You were right about Houston. It fuckin' sucks. I've been waiting for that *told ya so.* Is today the day I get it? "

"Nah." I chuckle. "Soon, though."

"Lookin' forward to it."

Then like lightning, an idea strikes me. "When you're done actin' like you're up and tootin' and decide to get your ass back to Valentine, I'll be happy to lease a piece of my new ranch to you. Could build your private practice there."

The line is so silent, I pull it away from my ear to make sure we didn't get disconnected. "Hello?"

"Sorry, I'm here. Are you serious?"

"Hell yeah, I am. As serious as a rattlesnake in the middle of a hiking trail."

He lets out a breath. "Wow. That would be fuckin' amazin'."

"Yeah, that sixty-mile drive is a pain in my ass. It's for selfish reasons and because I miss ya. But with that bein' said… my animals get dibs."

"Consider it done." I can hear the excitement in his voice, like he's thinking about the possibilities of it all just as much as me.

Before his mind wanders too much, I speak up. "There is one problem, though."

"Shit, I knew it was too good to be true."

"Kinda. Summer Jones wants the property, too."

Cash bursts into laughter. Not the reaction I was expecting, but I let him finish.

"Summer Jones? She's *still* bustin' your balls?"

I think about the way she nearly killed me with her dirty looks at the Mexican restaurant. "Somethin' like that."

"I don't know why you two don't fuck it out and get this feud—or whatever it is you've had going on since high school—over with. It's obnoxiously obvious that you both want each other."

"Not. True." I think back, trying to remember when things ultimately changed between us.

"I'm lookin' forward to the day when I can happily deliver my *I told you so.*"

"Trust me, that day will *never* fuckin' come."

He clears his throat. "Whatever you say, Beck. But ya know, admitting you have a boner for her is much easier than constantly denying it."

I roll my eyes even though he can't see me. "Sure thing. I'll be sure to take advice from someone who spends more time with horses than women."

"Just admit you've always had a thing for her, and I'll drop it."

Summer comes to my mind. Her laughter. Her smile. Even her scowl and the way she curses me under her breath. "I'll admit this: Summer might seem like sunshine, but she's really hell on earth. There is no way it would *ever* work out between us."

Cash howls his laughter. "Can't wait to rub your nose in this bullshit. Ahh, it's gonna be glorious." He's gloating, and I let him because he's dead wrong.

"Yeah, yeah. Ya done? Some of us have real work to finish before the sun sets."

"Whatever you say. I hope you get that property. If ya do, our deal is on."

"Oh, I will. Summer can get bent."

He snickers. "Over your bed as you tug at her hair from behind."

"Fuck off." I end the call with the thought of that very image in the forefront of my mind.

7

SUMMER

*I*t's the beginning of May, and it's already hotter than hell outside. The sun is high in the sky, and I feel like it's boiling my skin off my body.

My phone buzzes in my pocket, and I see my dad calling. He's got impeccable timing, because I just finished reorganizing the tack room.

"Hey, sweetie, whatcha doin'?"

"Nothin'. Just finished up in the barn."

"Great, you wanna saddle up and meet me on the west side of the property by Horseshoe Creek? The Whitleys contacted me and said some of our cows are on their property."

"Shit, how'd that happen?"

"Not sure. I've got a few of the ranch hands checking the perimeter to see if we can quickly find how they escaped, but we gotta herd them back over."

"Yeah, I'll saddle up now. Give me about fifteen." I grab a lead rope and head to the pasture to catch Big Red. He's a quarter horse with the spirit of a wild stallion and always takes me on an adventure. Sometimes I need to get my blood pumping just to remind myself of this experience I'm living called life.

I click the lead rope on his halter, then tie him with a slipknot to one of the hooks in the entryway of the barn. Quickly, I brush him down, then throw on a saddle pad, then the saddle. Once he's cinched up and ready to go, I put the bit of the western bridle in his mouth and attach it behind his ears. After a soft pat on his neck, I put my feet into the stirrups and pull myself up. We take off down the trail that follows the property line of the Horseshoe Creek Ranch.

I keep my eyes focused in the distance, admiring its property and geography. I've never wanted anything so much. For the first time in my life, I can imagine something as big as having my own bed-and-breakfast, and it being mine. And then I remember Beckett. *Ugh.*

One thing about riding is it allows me to process my thoughts. When I was a kid, my parents would ground me from the horses and punish me with barn chores. It didn't work out how they wanted, though, because I even enjoyed the shit work.

I could've taught lessons just like the Valentines, and I still could, but I just helped my parents with odd jobs while dreaming about opening a bed-and-breakfast. I've always been afraid that if I got paid to do what I love, I'd start hating it. Kinsley calls that my limiting beliefs or some shit. I'm happy to help around the ranch in whatever capacity, mainly having fun caring for the horses and chickens while dreaming big.

As my mind wanders, Big Red spooks, taking a step back before bolting.

Wanna know what scared him? A damn lizard.

All I can do is hold on for dear life as he gallops as fast as the wind. I laugh when he moves to a trot and then back to a walk.

"It's okay, boy. It's fine. You could stomp that little thing to smoosh." He snorts as if he understands while he continues to calm down.

I move my attention back to the other side of the fence. In the distance, I see several cows with our branding—a sideways

J, for Lazy J Ranch—grazing like they own the place. Honestly, when that property is mine, I wouldn't mind letting Dad use the land. Hell, I might want to get into cattle trading, too.

When I look over, I see Dad riding up the hill on the other side. A big smile meets my face, and I kick my heels, causing Big Red to take off into a gallop. He loves to run. I keep the reins in my hand and my arms down, enjoying the wind blowing through my ponytail.

"Afternoon." Dad chuckles when Big Red forces himself to a walk. "Did you spot 'em?"

"Yeah, they're over there." I point in that direction. "About six or seven cows."

"Yeah, that's what the Whitleys said. Guess we should round 'em up. I found the problem with the fence. Rotted post laid down flat, and they just walked right over it."

I shake my head. "Of course they did."

"I got the guys comin' to fix it up, just need to get those cows over here. Ready?"

"Yep," I say, and we find the opening that leads to the other part of the property and then start our roundup. Dad approaches the cows from one side, and I move from the other, but they're stubborn.

"It's times like this I wish we had a herding dog." I look at Dad, a reminder I've given him at least five times in the last few weeks.

"I'll consider it."

We work the cattle, and eventually, they start moving in the right direction. The goal is to keep them together and moving forward, but I know at any moment, one can bolt off, and the rest will follow. Thankfully, that doesn't happen.

The leader of the Angus cows lifts her head. "Moooo!"

I shake my head. "Assholes. Every last one of them."

Dad chuckles. "So about the property. What'd the bank say?"

I suck in a deep breath. "I got a call this mornin'. They said I'll need a cosigner."

"Your mom and I said we'd help, but that's risky." Dad stares off in the distance, then turns his head to meet my gaze.

"I know. I didn't even want to ask, because I couldn't imagine something happenin' and puttin' y'all in a bad situation."

Dad nods, and he's wearing a contemplative expression. "You believe in this bed-and-breakfast?"

"Yes. I *know* it'll be successful, and I won't let it fail. If it didn't do well, I'd sell the ranch and get it out from under y'all."

The silence draws on, and I'm sure he's going to say no.

But...then he smiles. "Okay then. You've helped so much with the cattle trading business and keeping me organized, Summer. I know you'll be successful, sweetie. If you want this, your mama and I will do whatever you need."

"Seriously?" My eyes are as wide as saucers. "You mean it?"

"Yeah, we believe in your vision, Summer. We want you to be successful but also work for it. Over the years, you've proven yourself. I know you'll have your hands full and will be busy, but that's a lesson everyone needs in life."

"Thank you, Daddy!" I nearly squeal. I'm overcome with emotions and try my hardest not to cry tears of joy, but a few stream down my cheeks anyway.

"What're the emotions for?" Dad searches my face, not used to the tears. I've never seen the man cry once. Not during his brother's funeral and not during my Grandpa's. I was raised to be tough as nails, but I still shed a few tears every once in a while.

"I'm just happy. But it ain't gonna be all sunshine and rainbows. Beckett Valentine wants the property too, and he's more than determined to give me a run for my money."

Dad chuckles. Everyone else gives me a hard time about Beckett, and I'm just glad Dad keeps things like that to himself.

"Give him hell." Dad leads the cows back onto our property just as a few ranch hands roll up on a four-wheeler with barbwire and a metal post strapped to the rack on the back.

"You know I will." I watch the lazy heifers mosey over the hill.

"Have the bank contact me. I'll go down there and sign."

"Thanks, Dad. I won't let you down."

"I know you won't."

On the ride back to the barn, I'm giddy with excitement. My parents' support is the only thing I need to ensure the Horseshoe Creek Ranch is mine.

Beckett motherfuckin' Valentine is going down.

I lead Big Red inside the stables and remove all the gear, brush him down, then let him loose. Immediately, he goes into the pasture and rolls around, coating his fresh-brushed fur with dirt. Then he bucks as he gallops away. He's my favorite asshole.

Considering I'm done for the day, I give Mom a call on the way home, which is only a short five-minute drive.

"Going to town after I shower. Need anything?"

"Hm."

I can hear her walking through the house, then I hear the fridge open. "Maybe some butter and a half gallon of vanilla ice cream."

"Sure thing. I'll drop it off in a couple of hours."

As soon as I walk inside my cabin, I kick off my boots and wiggle out of my jeans. I tear off my shirt and then remove my bra and panties before stepping into the shower. As I stand under the warm water, it washes away the sweat from the day and relaxes my muscles.

With my eyes closed, I think about Beckett and how he looked at Natalie at the restaurant. How his eyes seemed to peer straight through me. My hands guide down my body until my fingers graze my needy clit. I let out a moan as I rub slow circles.

"Fuck." I hiss, placing a leg on the side of the tub to give myself more access. I hate Beckett with every inch of my body, but that doesn't mean I don't want him. I wasn't kidding about the duct tape.

I slide one finger inside my tight, slick walls, wishing it were him filling me full. The man is sex on legs, gorgeous in his own way, with blue eyes and messy hair. A smirk that melts panties. He's built like steel, with muscles that go on for days, and his ass...damn. My nipples grow hard, and I pinch one, then tug as I insert another finger. My breathing increases, and a moan escapes me. One night. Maybe Kinsley is right, and that's all I'd need to get him out of my system. Live out the fantasy, then forget it ever happened. But I know it'd cause more problems than what it's worth.

I pick up my pace, moving between my dripping wet pussy and my clit, imagining Beckett's plump lips kissing and sucking my cunt. I bet he's good in bed. The women who've been with him have said as much. However, commitment isn't a word he knows, and I'll never become a notch on his headboard. Though, it's tempting.

Heat rushes throughout my body, and I'm close.

So fucking close.

But instead of coming, I pull away. I don't give myself the release my body begs for. I don't lose myself to thoughts of Beckett. I deserve to be punished for it because he's so bad for me. My clit is needy and swollen, and my pussy aches for more...but I hold off for now.

I grab my blueberry-scented body wash and loofah. When I wash between my legs, my body urges me to continue. Slowly, I tease my hard clit, nearly edging myself to oblivion before pulling away again. It's a game, all of it, one where I deny myself pleasure, teasing myself until my body completely crumbles to ash. It's what I deserve for wanting someone I shouldn't.

When I'm close, my breathing is ragged, and I pull away once again and then wash my hair. It's agonizing—the pulse between my legs, the hard nipples, the release begging to be set free—but it makes coming better. Considering no man in a one-hundred-mile radius can remotely please me.

I like it rough and hard and want to be fucked like I'm his own personal rag doll. I want to be spanked, brought to the edge over and over, and then told I can come when I'm hanging on by a single thread. Beckett drives me fuckin' wild.

I desperately want to be pleased inside and outside of the bedroom, and so far, I'm convinced it will never happen. Somehow though, I know that Beckett *could* get the job done if his big-ass ego weren't in the way. While I've secretly crushed on him since I was fourteen, I'd never admit it to anyone. Hell, I lie to myself every damn day. This shit with the Horseshoe Creek Ranch and inconveniently seeing him has caused all those old feelings I've been drowning for over a decade to resurface. And I hate it.

Once I'm clean, I step out of the shower, wrap a towel around my body, then lie down on my bed. Rolling to my side, I reach inside the drawer next to my bed and pull out one of my favorite toys that hit the G- and C-spot.

As soon as I press the button and click it on the lowest setting, the toy buzzes to life.

Closing my eyes, I slide it down my body, teasing myself. I'm so wet, and my back arches with delight as soon as it's inside. I quickly soar, my body begging for the release that I denied myself several times in the shower. I fantasize about Beckett and his strong hands and hard dick pumping me. Just the thought of his lips and tongue circling my clit has me teetering on edge. I can barely hold back the orgasm.

I groan out, rocking my hips, wishing his warm, strong body was making me lose control.

"Beckett," I whisper. Then as if a firework show explodes inside me, I'm coming. My muscles contract, and I groan in pleasure but don't stop. I keep it going, pumping it inside me while the top flicks against my clit.

"Fuck you, Beckett." The heat builds again. I'm suspended on edge until I let go and topple over it. When I masturbate to thoughts of him, I grow greedy, needing more than one orgasm. It always ends with two.

I turn off the toy, then glide my hand down to my pussy and insert two fingers.

Soaked. It happens any time I think about him like this. Then immediately after, the thought pisses me off.

I lie there with my eyes closed, trying to regain reality. Eventually, I do, then I get dressed and grab my keys. When I walk down the porch of my modest cabin, I try to ignore the still-dead plants with the decaying stalks, then remove the soft top from the Jeep.

This afternoon, I'm allowing the warm breeze and wind to dry my hair naturally.

Once I'm in town, I pull into the nursery parking lot and see the hot pink and purple flowers. It's a shame that whatever I'll buy today will die, but I'm going to give it my good-ole-girl try. I grab an empty cart from the parking lot and wheel it inside. As soon as I'm under the gigantic greenhouse covering, Vera sees me and walks over. She looks so much like Kinsley when we were sixteen, it's almost scary. Then again, all the Valentine girls look the same.

"Summer!" She's wearing a big grin. "What happened to the flowers you bought last week?"

Her blue eyes meet mine. Vera's gorgeous and sweet, and she also loves plants. She's like a Disney princess living in a beautiful garden who can grow anything because she has a magical green thumb. Her tomatoes and squash are to die for. The best I've ever had.

"I don't know! I did everything you said. Direct sunlight. Water often. They just…*died*."

She snickers. "I'm starting not to believe any of this. There's just no way."

"I agree with you! At this point, I better never have kids, because I can't even keep a plant alive for a week."

Vera shakes her head. "So what are you tryin' this week?"

"I dunno. Maybe you can sell me something that I literally can't kill."

Vera chuckles. "If anyone could kill an unkillable plant, it's you, Summer. I gave you Texas mountain laurels. They thrive in West Texas."

I groan. "I'm doomed, aren't I?"

"Probably." She shrugs. "Have you ever thought about pursuing another hobby?"

"No, I'm too far committed at this point. I guess I should start namin' these plants. Maybe I'll take it more seriously."

"Anything is worth trying. Don't want ya to go broke on this habit of yours." She winks, leading me over to the succulents. "These can basically survive the apocalypse."

I look over them. "But they're not…*cute*."

"Sure they are! Look, you can choose different ones. Mix and match."

"I'm buying more flowers."

Vera playfully pats my back. "Good. I like seeing you every other week. When you stop killing plants, it'll be impossible to run into you with my school and work schedule."

I grin wide. "That's true. But hey, once I buy the Horseshoe Creek Ranch, I'm probably gonna need some help running the B&B. You know you've always got a job if you need one."

She wraps her arms around me and hugs me. "Thank you! But ya know my brother also offered me a job at the new training facility. I guess I win either way."

"At least one of us does. I'm gonna miss you if you stop

workin' here anytime soon." The only time I get to visit with her is at the nursery.

"You don't have to worry about that. This place doesn't even feel like a job."

A woman needs help across the way, and Vera excuses herself as I look over the lantana flowers. They're bright red and would be perfect in front of my cabin. I bend over to smell them, and when I straighten up and step back, I nearly run into a brick wall. Or so I thought.

Beckett.

"Have you ever heard of personal space?" I glare at him, stepping to the side to create much-needed space between us.

He smirks, meeting my gaze, but the fire in his eyes tells me he's unamused. "Have you ever heard of payin' attention?"

My mouth straightens into a firm line. "What are you doin' here, anyway?"

I've seen him more in the last week than I have all month. It's easier to forget he exists when I don't have to look at the gorgeous asshole.

"Oh, just lookin' around, plannin' how I'll landscape the new stables I'm buildin' at Horseshoe Creek."

Just hearing him talk about it like it's already his infuriates the shit out of me. "Over my dead body."

He leans in close, and the intoxicating smell of his cologne mixed with sweat nearly does me in. His voice lowers. "You know what you need, SumSum?"

I strongly dislike him calling me that.

"To get laid every once in a while. Might help ya not be so damn angry all the fuckin' time."

Heat rushes to my cheeks, remembering the orgasms that overtook me as I thought about his stupid but sexy ass. I can't stand how my body instantly reacts to his closeness like it has a mind of its own.

"Don't call me that."

Beckett pulls away, chuckling. Of course, he notices how flushed I am. He's always had that effect on me. "Loosen up."

I find my words. "Go to hell."

"Sure will. And I'll see you there." He reaches forward, grabs one of the pots of lantanas, and walks away.

I hate the fact that I love to watch him go.

8

BECKETT

*I*t's been three days since I last saw Summer, and I'm pretty sure she'd have murdered me if she could. Right now, she's the only other person interested in the ranch, so it's my priority to stay in the know.

Last night, I took Natalie out to dinner again. We went to the deli in town and had soup and sandwiches, where she confirmed I still have the highest bid. If no one beats me, her grandfather has agreed to sell it for that price.

It feels good to be victorious, to get what I want, and to have earned it fair and square.

I know winning means Summer will probably hate me for life, but that was bound to happen anyway. So it's not that big of a loss. Eventually, she'll get over it. Or maybe she won't. Seems she's been holding the same grudge against me since high school.

After getting dressed, I grab my keys and head to my parents' house. A few times per month, the entire family gets together and has dinner so we can catch up with one another. Once the older kids started moving out and getting jobs off the ranch, Mama made it a rule that we still had to visit. We're family, and the family that eats together, sticks together. Her saying, not mine.

When I pull up to the big farmhouse, I realize I'm late. Like ridiculously late. Cars and trucks are parked haphazardly on the side of the long driveway, and I pull off into the grass and then make my way inside. As soon as I open the door, I smell fresh tomatoes, basil, and garlic. My stomach rumbles with anticipation because I know she made one of my favorite meals—spaghetti and meatballs. I enter the kitchen, and everyone is here except for Kinsley.

I laugh, happy I wasn't the rotten egg this time. She's going to be pissed.

Mom, Dad, Mawmaw Valentine, and Papa Valentine are at one end of the table. Then Harrison, Colt, Emmett, and Sterling are sitting on one side. My sisters Remi, Fenix, London, and Vera are on the other.

"Where the hell is Kinsley?"

My siblings burst into *oooohs* and start pointing.

"I'm right here!" She walks up behind me, huffing like she sprinted inside. "I was hoping that I wouldn't be the last one here, but I guess I'm doing the damn dishes tonight."

It's one of Mom's rules. We all arrive early to eat on time, or the last one has clean-up duty. And with fourteen people, it sucks.

Harrison howls with laughter. "Show up early, then there's no way you're doing bitch work!"

"Language!" Mawmaw wags her finger. "My ancient ears won't put up with it."

"Ancient? Grandma, you're not *that* old." Vera bats her long eyelashes at her.

Remi leans closer to her. "Suck-up."

"Honey, when your knees start poppin', age don't even matter."

Colt looks at me. "That's what she said."

I shake my head. I love my brothers and sisters, but we tend to get into a lot of trouble together.

Only two seats are left at the table, which puts Kinsley and me right next to each other. We're not necessarily on the best terms right now because of all this ranch stuff, but I'll put it all aside tonight.

We sit, then Dad and Papa bring out two large army-sized pots of spaghetti. Fenix is the middle child of the ten of us, and she grabs silverware and begins passing it around just as Sterling, my youngest brother, sets two huge loaves of homemade garlic bread on each end. Vera and Sterling still live at home, and the rest of us have our own places. However, it's a mixed bag with who works on the ranch and who doesn't.

Keeps it interesting, to say the least.

As soon as Emmett reaches forward and cuts a piece of bread, then pops it into his mouth, my mom lets out her child-wrangling whistle that nearly pierces ears. It's how she'd round us up as kids, and even hearing it today causes panic to spark inside me. That whistle was sometimes worse than a whooping.

"Can we at least say grace first?" Mom glares in his direction, and he gulps down the food.

"Damn, you've done it now." Harrison shakes his head at him, but all he does is shrug while he chews.

"I'm starving. Dear Jesus. Thanks for the food. Blessings and love. Blah-blah. Let's eat!"

Mawmaw gasps.

I meet his eyes. "You're gonna make them both blow a damn gasket."

This is typical when we get together. Too many different personalities, but at the core, we're pretty much the same. We're Valentines, after all.

Once the lids are removed from the pots, we begin filling our plates. The sounds of forks against plates are all that can be heard. When our mouths are full, it's pretty much the only time we're all quiet.

Kinsley glances at me as she chews and swallows the garlic bread she just popped into her mouth. "So." She takes a long pause. "When're ya gonna give up the ghost and decide you're not buyin' that property next door?"

I laugh, but it's sarcastic. "That's absolutely *not* happening."

Mawmaw looks in my direction. "You're buying the Horseshoe Creek Ranch? I thought that was a rumor."

"Everyone thinks it is. It's not. I'm buyin' it. Already started contacting contractors to get quotes for building a brand-new training facility."

My brothers and sisters all chime in with words of encouragement, and so do the elder Valentines. Everyone seems to be beaming with excitement and positivity. Everyone except for Kinsley. I shoot her a smirk, but she's seething.

"You're not stopping me, Kins. Give it up."

She sets her fork down on the side of her plate, causing a clanking sound. "You're such an asshole!"

"Language." Mawmaw is ready to snap, but Kinsley continues.

"You know for a fact Summer wants to buy that property to open a bed-and-breakfast. It's been her lifelong dream since we were kids. You can train *anywhere*."

"And she can open a B&B somewhere else."

Her teeth are gritted closed. "No, she can't."

Harrison raises his hand. "I have an idea. Why don't you just marry Summer since you two are destined to be together, and then the problem is solved? You'd both own it."

"No." I leave out the cussing so I don't set Grandma off, but damn, it's hard.

"Yeah, that's a great idea." Kinsley pops a brow.

"Now you're both being ridiculous."

Vera clears her throat. "Well…I saw the way you two looked at each other at the nursery the other day."

"I don't know what you're talkin' about."

Colt and Remi, the twins, start singing. "Summer and Beckett sitting in a tree…"

I try to ignore everyone as they talk over each other.

"Enough!" Dad holds up his hand. "Enough from the peanut gallery. Y'all settle down. Beckett will admit he has a crush when he's ready."

"To be very clear, I don't. And I won't be sharing that property with *anyone* other than this dumba—idiot, because we're moving our business next door. There's more room for opportunity."

Harrison puffs out his chest, flashing his million-dollar smile. I turn to Kinsley. "So *stop* being delusional."

Papa interrupts us. "Kins, how's the job at the newspaper goin'?"

She stabs at a meatball. "Oh, you know, the same as it has since 1910, considerin' Mr. Anderson is running the paper into the ground."

"He's a nice guy." Grandma smiles.

"No, he's not. He's horrible."

I look over at Colt. "How's the handyman work goin' for ya?"

It's been a couple of weeks since we've talked. Last year, he started helping people with their honey-do lists, and ever since then, he's been busy as hell using his carpentry skills.

"It's been a lot. Yesterday, I built a water well shack for Mr. Porter over on Skylight Drive in an hour. Painted an entire house last week. All I gotta say is it's never boring. There are always different tasks to do, and the money is pretty good. Havin' fun."

I smile. "Proud of ya, bro."

"Why don't you ever say that to me?" Harrison takes a huge bite of spaghetti and chews with his mouth open.

I shake my head.

London chats about her online college work. It was something she decided she wanted to pursue right after high school. She moved away for college for one year, then swiftly returned and changed all her classes to online. She's been much happier since. I don't think any of us are cut out for the fast-paced city life. She's smart and kind, and she'll be unstoppable once she figures out what she wants to do in life.

Forks eventually stop moving, and Dad picks up the empty plates. Sterling helps clean the table as Fenix and Vera chat about the garden.

"The sauce was made from the tomatoes I grew."

"Wow." I stand to stretch. "You've got such a little green thumb."

"Have you tried the zucchini this season yet? Mama fried some up last week."

"You fried zucchini and didn't tell us?" Colt glares at Mom.

She shrugs. "Slipped my mind."

"It was amazin'." Sterling rubs it in.

I turn back to Vera. "I grabbed a few tomatoes last week, and they were good. I'll have to raid your garden and make some if they're *that* great."

"Don't be stealin' all the veggies." Grandma walks up and hugs me. "I've missed ya, Beck. You don't come around so often no more."

"Just been busy, Mawmaw. I know it's hard not seeing your favorite grandkid."

She snickers.

"You're all my favorite." She speaks loudly so everyone hears but then shoots me a wink.

"Ya never forget the first, though."

Once the table is cleared, Kinsley makes quick work of washing the dishes. I almost feel bad for her, but considering she tried me earlier, I don't offer to help. She deserves dish duty for fourteen.

Papa announces the pies will be ready in ten minutes as the scent of apples and cinnamon fills the house. I'm so full I don't think I can eat another bite, but I won't pass up Mawmaw's dessert. So when I'm handed a slice along with a large scoop of vanilla Blue Bell ice cream, I take it and don't feel a lick of regret eating it.

"You should sell these." I shove a big spoonful into my mouth.

She grins. "Maybe I will. How many you wanna buy?"

"No way, I get the family discount."

"Ain't nothin' for free." She laughs.

I look around the room that's full of family and smile.

"So when ya gonna find a partner and get married?" Papa meets my gaze.

"Never."

"I'd like to be a great-grandma before I'm eighty." Mawmaw meets my eyes, putting pressure on me.

"You have nine other people you can hassle."

Mom clears her throat. "Vera is sixteen, and Sterling is still in high school. London has already said she's not dating anyone until she graduates from college. So that leaves seven if we're gettin' specific."

"And we're not." Emmett picks up his fork. "I'm not ready for all that."

"Me neither," Colt, Fenix, and Remi say at the same time.

"I might be able to make some babies happen." Harrison waggles his brows, and Grandma literally shakes her head.

I burst into laughter. "No one is ready for those hellions. But who knows, you might have some runnin' around out there already."

"Doubt it. I double wrap—"

"Okay, okay. We get it." Dad holds up his hand.

Kinsley sighs. "I'm a single pringle."

"There's always Hayden."

Her face immediately turns furious, and she narrows her eyes at me. "Who?"

She has this thing where she likes to pretend her ex doesn't exist, but I know better. If she wants to constantly bring up Summer at the most inappropriate times, I'll return the favor.

"Hayden Shaw. Your ex. Don't recall?"

"No. I don't."

Then all eyes are back on me. "Good chat, y'all. Super helpful." The sarcasm isn't lost.

Considering I have to be up early, I decide to leave once we finish dessert. Mom usually makes coffee, and we sit around discussing our lives, but after dinner, there's nothing else for me to say.

I hug everyone goodbye, and honestly, if I knew I wouldn't get shunned for it, I'd have just waved and left. On the way to my truck, Kinsley catches up with me.

"Way to start shit back there." I keep my eyes forward and my pace steady as she falls in line beside me.

As she forcefully shoves her hands into her dress pants pockets. "You know Summer's dream has always been to open a B&B, and you're wrong for taking that from her."

"I'm not taking anything from her, Kinsley. I'm just not putting *her* first. For once, I'm thinking about myself and my career. I'm your older brother. It was just you and me for a short time in our lives. I remember when you wanted the best for me and my future. So how about you be my sister and support me occasionally instead of worrying about your friend who'd run over me with her Jeep if she had the chance."

She meets my eyes, studying me for a moment as we continue walking. I didn't realize how far away we had to park, but considering we both showed up late, it's to be expected.

"You just don't get it, do you? *You* don't *need* that property to be successful in your training business. Everything is already in place, with room to expand right here. Maybe if you'd step outside of your own ego every once in a while and see how much depends on this, you'd fuckin' get it. Her opening that B&B benefits your business and the entire town, you selfish asshole. Hopefully, one day you'll consider doing the right thing for once. But I guess that day's not today." She takes a breath. "Oh, and when you start acting like my big brother who gives a shit about other people, then I'll start treating you like him."

Kinsley picks up her pace and walks past me. I suck in a deep breath and let her go. The last thing I want to do is argue. I'm mentally and physically exhausted. And she's right, I hadn't considered any of those things, but I also don't deserve her attitude.

The opportunity to buy the land is the same for everyone. It's not my fault my bid is higher.

As Kinsley drives off, I almost stop her, but it's better if I don't. She's not a grudge holder, at least not when it comes to family—ex-boyfriends are a completely different story—so I know she'll eventually get over this. Meanwhile, she's given me a lot to think about.

Either way, I'm not lying down for a woman who'd prefer me as roadkill. Now if she were nicer, maybe. But we all know Summer Jones ain't a ray of fuckin' sunshine, especially when it comes to me.

9

SUMMER

*M*y phone buzzes in my pocket, and I pull it out to see Kinsley calling me. Ever since this property debacle started with her brother, she's made keeping me informed a priority. And damn, I love her for it.

"What's the scoop?" I stack empty buckets in the feed room.

"Can you meet Natalie at Grindin' Beans around noon?"

"Today?"

"Yeah, I thought maybe you could submit your offer in person. Maybe then you can read her reaction. She seems very easy to read. Anyway, who knows, maybe she'll give you some insider information or something."

I laugh. "Kins, people don't just offer info up to me like they do for you. But I do need to submit my offer. I've been doing a lot of research on ranch prices based on what my parents' property is worth and all of that. I'm just worried."

"Don't be, girl! You've got this. Remember, gotta believe it to receive it!"

I love how positive and energetic she is about this, but I just hope she's right.

"Thanks for being my woo-woo cheerleader." I chuckle.

"When the B&B is ready, I'm going to have a windowsill dedicated to charging all those crystals I'm going to have when I turn into a believer."

She snickers. "Better be a big window, that's all I'm saying. I have a serious collection on my desk right now. You might think it's cheesy, but there's nothing like clear quartz to help me manifest everything I want."

"Clear quartz? I have no idea what that is."

"Google is your friend! But anyway, today, when you show up at the coffee shop, pretend you just happen to be there. Her favorite drink is a mocha latte with no whipped cream. Order the same thing, and you'll have something to help you start the conversation."

"Thanks, coach."

"You're welcome."

She knows sometimes I can be awkward as hell, especially when it comes to striking up random conversations. I'm friendly, sure, but I also like to get straight to the point with business. I've been brought into too many hour-long conversations about random things going on in town because I'm also too polite to walk away. "The things you learn never fail to amaze me."

"It's why you keep me around." There's a smile in her voice. "Well, that aaaaaand because you've got a huge crush on my brother."

"Respectfully, he can go fuck himself."

"Perfect answer. Anyway, I gotta go. Mr. Anderson is walkin' over, and I need to pretend I'm workin' on this article about the Fourth of July celebration."

"Sounds good. I'll keep you updated! Wish me luck."

"Sending all the good juju your way."

"Right back atcha." I end the call and check the time. I have an hour to shower off the morning and naturally arrive at the coffee shop. Pretending to run into her will be the hard part because I'm not an actress by any means. I tend to wear my heart on my sleeve, and what you see is what you get, but I'll do what I have to do.

Kinsley typically knows best when it comes to social situations, especially with things like this, and I can use all the help I can get.

After I'm dressed and presentable, I slip on my running shoes and then fill out the paperwork to make the official bid for the ranch. My heart pounds hard in my chest as I write down the number.

Two Million.

It's a fair offer. I just hope it's enough.

I suck in a deep breath, tuck the paper into the envelope, and seal it with a wish before heading out the door.

On the way to the coffee shop, I practice what I'll say and the surprised tone in my voice. She seems like a nice person, even if she couldn't stop eye-fucking Beckett. But then again, it's not her fault. He has that effect on women.

When I arrive, I notice her grandfather's truck parked up front, and I shake my head at how accurate Kinsley's timing is. My best friend has a way of getting information about people in the easiest way. It's why she's so good at her job at the newspaper.

As soon as I enter, the cowbell above the door dings loudly. Immediately, I'm greeted by Jessica. She's in her midtwenties, and her parents own the place, but it will be hers one day. She gives me a big hello and a smile. I go to the counter and do exactly as Kinsley instructed.

"Hey, Summer! Been a while since I've seen ya around. How're things at the ranch?"

"They're great. Enjoyin' the nice weather we're having. Glad it's finally warmin' up."

It's typical to talk about the weather, plus it's easy to complain about it being too hot or too cold. Someone always has an opinion about the temperature around here.

"Yeah, I feel the same way. So whatcha havin'?"

I look up at the menu and see she added a few new things. "Ooh, lavender mocha?"

"It's so good. So is the lavender matcha."

I laugh. "Matcha tastes like hay to me."

She smiles wide. "I never thought of it like that. But yeah, I can see the similarities. Sure does smell like hay."

My eyes slide down the menu like I'm trying to make up my mind. "I think I'm gonna get a large mocha latte, no whipped cream, please." When I turn my head, I see Natalie busy on her laptop by the window that oversees the sidewalk. She's typing away and doesn't even lift her head, but since the café is somewhat empty, I know she heard. But she doesn't pay me any attention.

"Perfect." Jessica grabs a cup and punches it into her computer. "I'll fix it up for ya and meet you down at the other end."

"Great." I slide her my card, then walk to the other side of the long counter. The beans start grinding in the espresso machine, and then the smell of espresso fills my nose. I'm looking forward to this fancy coffee, considering I've been drinking Folgers all week. Nothing wrong with it. It does the job and jolts me awake in the morning, but it's not the strongest.

Jessica finishes, slides a cardboard sleeve around my to-go cup, and hands it over. "Enjoy!"

"Thanks, have a good one." I spin on my heels, suck in a deep breath, then make my way over to Natalie, wearing my best smile.

"Hi!" It comes out a little too peppy, but then again, I'm nervous. "I was just getting ready to call you to put in my offer."

Her plump, probably filled lips turn up as she meets my eyes. "What a lucky coincidence. Have a seat. I was just taking care of some work. This place has the best Wi-Fi in the area."

"Oh yeah, it does. Out at the ranch, it's terrible."

"Girl, you're telling me. I'd be better off sending smoke

signals than an email out there. Not sure how you guys survive."

I laugh in all the right places. "Honestly, I don't either. I think we're just used to it taking ten years to load a web page."

She takes a sip of her coffee, and I see her drink order written on the side.

"You like the mocha lattes, too?" I hold up mine.

"It's the best drink I think I've ever had in my life. I come here every day around this time and order it. When I go back to Florida, I'm going to miss this little routine."

I nod. I'd bet my last dollar that Kinsley saw her here and started chatting, and that was how she knew she'd be here. She's so smart but also sly.

"I can imagine. But I'm sure you miss not being home."

"Yeah, kinda. It's just easier when you have access to everything. When I get back home, I will not be taking Chipotle, tanning salons, or a twenty-four-hour gym for granted ever again."

I smile but don't relate. The two of us are not the same.

"So about that bid." I pull the envelope from my back pocket and hand it to her.

"Oh yeah." She takes it from me and opens it, then meets my eyes. "Thanks for this! I'll make sure to show it to Grandpa, and I'll be in touch after he makes his decision."

Her tone isn't very convincing, so I find the courage to speak up. "Is it not enough?"

Natalie meets my eyes. "All I can say is it's lower than the other offers we've received. I can't tell you what the number should be because it's a closed bidding process."

My heart hammers hard in my chest. The excitement I felt chatting with Kinsley about crystals and everything else vanishes, and the dream fades away. It's replaced with sadness and a touch of anger. *Fuckin' Beckett.*

"Thank you." I try to keep my tone even, covering the defeat. "Can I submit another offer?"

"Absolutely. Grandpa won't close the bidding until the end of the month."

I smile. "Thank you for everything."

"You're welcome! Good luck, Summer."

"Thanks. Apparently, I'm gonna need it."

She grins.

I grab my cup and stand. "See ya 'round."

I have a little over two weeks to make a decision. As soon as I leave the coffee shop, my forced smile drops off my face. I'm a whirlwind of emotions as I climb inside my Jeep and text Kinsley.

> My bid is too low.

> FUCK! I'm ANGRY!

Just remember, everything always works out. Did she tell you how much you need to increase it by?

> No.

I don't even want to have this conversation right now, and Kinsley doesn't deserve the attitude, either.

I'm in a bad mood. I don't want to overpay for the land. If I only knew what offer your stupid brother made, then I'd know how much higher I need to go. He's making my life difficult AF!

Don't give up. It's not over until the fat lady sings.

> Right now, you're the only person who believes in miracles. I'm wasting too much energy on this for it not to work out in the end.

> Deep down in my gut, I know this is yours. I can't explain it to you, but sometimes I know things. Your business will be there. And I can't wait to celebrate with you when that happens.

> You know, toxic positivity is a thing.

> There isn't anything toxic about this. I promise you, one way or another, the Whitleys' big-ass house is going to be yours. You'll be cookin' those famous chocolate chip cookies your mama makes and pancakes every morning. And it will be successful. Mark my words. And then later, when it happens, I get to give you your own personalized Valentine I told you so.

I roll my eyes. The Valentines are all too cocky for their own good. However, Kinsley's track record is pretty high.

> I'm going to buy more plants to kill. I'll text you when I get home.

> Why don't you stick with fake ones? That way, you just gotta worry about the sun making them fade.

I laugh, and I realize how much I needed it.

> One of these days, I'm going to figure out how not to kill a plant. Plus, retail therapy helps.

> I understand that! Now, remember…no diggity, no doubts. It's yours!

> We'll see.

I send the last message, then drive a few blocks over and

stop at the nursery. Vera is at school, so the owner helps me. He's almost shocked when he sees how many plants I have in my cart.

"What's the occasion?" he asks, ringing up all the flowers.

"I'm planning a funeral."

He gives me a look.

"I'm kidding. I'm just being morbid because I'm not getting my way. You know how it goes."

"Sure." He shoots me a friendly grin. "You need someone to help you with this?"

"Nah, I got it." I need the distraction of doing something to clear my mind. I swipe my debit card, then walk to the Jeep and unload everything into the back. Wanting some fresh air, I remove the top, allowing the sunshine to bake me on the way home. With my hands on the steering wheel, I think about that property, and my subconscious leads me to one of the pull-offs in front of the Horseshoe Creek Ranch.

I get out of the Jeep and lean against the door, trying to visualize the big ten-bedroom house in the distance completely remodeled. I think about the landscaping I'd try my best to do and the lighting I'd have installed at the entrance to illuminate the sign everyone would have to drive under. The faded white house has cracked and chipped paint right now. It needs a good pressure washing, but the bones are incredible.

The place was built during the Great Depression by the original owners of the property, and at this point, it should have its own historical marker. I can imagine it painted light gray with white trim.

I suck in a deep breath and close my eyes as the warm breeze brushes against my skin.

What's meant to happen will happen.

While I'll try my damnedest to win it, I can't let this consume me any more than it already has the past few days.

As I stare out into the distance, I place my hand on my heart. "If it's meant to be, let it be."

The fluffy white clouds lazily drift across the sky, and I throw my wish to the universe. If Kinsley believes in this stuff, maybe it won't hurt if I do too. The worst that can happen is nothing will change. My life isn't so bad, and I have much to be grateful for.

But I want what's rightfully mine, and I'm willing to work and fight for it.

As I take in another deep breath, I hear the roar of an engine in the distance. Glancing over, I see a big Ram truck pulling off into the grass and parking right in front of my Jeep.

When I meet Beckett's deep-blue eyes, frustration rolls through me in waves.

He shoots me a smirk, and I audibly groan.

"As if today couldn't get any worst." I force my hands into my pockets so I'm not tempted to knock him out.

He gives me a smug look. "Ya know, I was thinkin' the same damn thing."

10

BECKETT

"*W*hat're ya doin' here? Admirin' my beautiful soon-to-be property?"

Her lips straighten into a firm line. "Why're you doin' this to me?"

I move closer to her. "Please. Don't flatter yourself, Summer. Have you ever stopped to think that not everything I do is to get back at you?"

"No. For as long as I can remember, you've taken one hundred percent of the possible shots fired."

I laugh. "That's not true."

"Okay, ninety-five percent."

"That's more accurate." With each passing second, I can tell she's growing pissed, but I enjoy seeing her worked up like this. Reminds me of how much spunk she has. "But to be real with ya, I have my own dreams and aspirations, too. This property..." I gaze into the distance and see the big house. "It's not personal."

"Hell yes, it is. It's *very* personal." She gives me a smug look.

"It's *not*. We just happen to want the same thing."

A sarcastic laugh releases from her. "Yeah, for the first time in our lives. How fuckin' convenient! Tell me how much your offer is." She's being stern, more than usual, and I realize she's actually mad.

"That's a no." I glance at her, giving her the same attitude right back.

She breaks our eye contact and focuses on the house. It's the perfect size and location for a bed-and-breakfast, and I do somewhat hate taking this from her.

Kinsley's words come to mind, but I push them away. Right now isn't the time to have a damn conscience, not when so much is on the line.

"I need to know if I even have a shot at this, Beckett." My name is like poison on her lips.

"Okay…I'll tell you. *If*—"

"Of course you have stipulations." She shakes her head.

"Go on a date with me."

Her head whips around. "You can't be serious."

"Do I look like I'm jokin'? Just one date."

"I'm not playing into your game so that you can humiliate me *again*."

The last word lingers in the air. *Again.*

I'm reminded of that time during my senior year when Summer was dating a guy my age who was on the rodeo team. He was too old for her. Too much of a fuckin' creep and was trying to take advantage of her naivety, age, and beauty.

I've tried to forget that night on many occasions, and here it's being mentioned nearly fifteen years later. One day, I will break down her walls, and maybe she'll talk about it. Today isn't the time, though.

"I've never *tried* to humiliate you, SumSum. I like to give you a hard time, just like I give to Kinsley."

She narrows her eyes at me. "I'm not your sister, Beckett. Remember that. And stop calling me that stupid nickname."

How could I forget when she's the only woman who's ever dug herself so far under my skin that she's left an imprint on my soul? "So about that date."

"No." She stands firm, shooting me her signature death glare. It'd almost be frightening if she intimidated me. I find it cute when she's this mad. We've gone back and forth with each other since we were preteens. Could be another reason why she hates me so much.

"Scared you'll have fun?"

She gives me another pointed look and places her hand over her chest. "Are you so desperate that you want to date someone who can't stand you? Bless your heart."

I can tell I'm getting to her. Good, I love returning the favor.

"I'm leaving now. Get your big fuckin' truck out of my way."

"You can reverse, sweetie." Sarcasm drips from my tone as she climbs into her Jeep. The top is down, and so are the windows, so it's not much of an escape from me.

"So that's a firm no, then?"

"That's right."

I shrug, unaffected by her snub. I lean against the door and smile. "You'll never be able to outbid me without knowing my number. What if you offer too much? Or too little? Those things would haunt you at night, wouldn't they? Wouldn't it be terrible to lose to little ole me?" Right now, I'm taunting her on purpose. No more playing nice.

"Fuck off." She jerks the Jeep in reverse, but she doesn't take her foot off the brakes, at least not yet.

"When you decide not to be so stubborn, text me. I'll be waiting."

Her green-as-emerald eyes meet mine, and she takes her foot off the brake, reversing so fast she kicks up gravel and dust. I cross my arms over my chest and chuckle as she sticks her middle finger into the air. My focus stays on her until the road curves and she's out of sight. Then I reach down and adjust my hard cock. She tends to do that to me.

The way her eyes slide up and down my body isn't lost on

me. How her nipples grow hard and her breath grows ragged anytime I'm close. Summer Jones may act as if she hates me, but a part of her secretly wants me, too.

A part of her wants me as much as I want her. We're both just too stubborn to admit it. One date could change the whole trajectory of our relationship, but she's too bullheaded to give me a chance.

At this point, I'm not even sure she's submitted an offer yet.

I make a mental note to text Natalie and ask if she's received any more bids. She won't tell me specifics, but she'll give me the information I need to know. As long as this competition stays between Summer and me, owning the ranch is in my near future. I've asked several people I thought might be interested, but everyone has supported me since it's right next to my parents' land. Sixteen days and the bidding closes.

Before climbing into my truck and driving away, I take it all in.

There is enough land to make it worth my while, and it would give me the space I need to expand. I can hire more trainers, Harrison can take on all the lessons, and we can take this highly successful business to the next level. Just thinking about it makes me smile.

My phone buzzes in my pocket, and I see it's Cash, so I answer. "What's up?"

"Nothin' much. Just leavin' work and was thinkin' about what you said last week."

I smile. "I'm standing outside the Horseshoe Creek Ranch now. I'll send you a pic."

"Yeah? Did you get it?" He sounds excited.

"Not yet, but soon. Just competing with Summer. Pretty sure this is gonna turn into a bidding war."

"Ya think?"

"Oh yeah. She's too determined. Wanted to know what my offer was."

"Did you tell her?" He sounds intrigued.

"Hell no. I didn't tell her shit. I offered to if she went on a date with me."

Cash howls with laughter. "No, you didn't. And let me guess, she said no?"

"Of course, she said no. I'd probably have dropped dead from shock if she'd said yes."

He chuckles. "Glad you finally decided to stop being so chickenshit and put on your big boy boxers and asked her out. Even if it's with stipulations."

"It's the only way she'd ever agree to it. She needs this more than I do."

"You sure about that?"

I think about his question for a moment. "Pretty confident."

"Well, keep me updated. If you win, I'm movin' home and opening my business there. I miss my parents and my sisters. Houston is far away. Makes coming home to visit hard, and we're not gettin' any younger."

"Great, man. You'll be the first to know. But damn, the pressure."

He sighs. "I know. Sorry about that, *kinda*. Just don't be a loser."

"Never am."

"Good."

Another call comes in, so he lets me go.

I think about everything and wasn't kidding about the pressure, though. Cash is one of my oldest friends, and we grew up doing everything together. When he moved away, I immediately felt the loss, and it would be like old times having him around again. Sure, we both have real responsibilities now, but at least we could hang out on the weekends and shoot the breeze. However, that means more is riding on this than just my future. Cash's and Harrison's are too.

Sucking in a deep breath, I climb into my truck and make my way home. Summer has me so worked up that as soon as I walk inside my house, I go to the shower.

I lather myself with soap and stand under the hot water, allowing the stream to pound against my skin. Roughly, I tug my dick, which is aching for release.

"Fuck." I stroke myself, the soap allowing my hand to glide swiftly up and down my shaft. Summer's sassy mouth is on my mind, and I'd love to shove my cock so far down her throat that she chokes on it. Imagining her naked and on her knees, begging for me like the goddess she is, nearly sends me over the top.

The orgasm quickly builds, and deep grunts release from me as my balls tighten. I place my palm flat against the shower wall, stroking my cock slow and hard until I lose myself to the thoughts of Summer. She's so gorgeous, and that smart mouth of hers gets me so worked up. Fighting with her is the best aphrodisiac there is, and I honestly have no regrets. She'll come around, or maybe she won't. Seems like I win something either way.

11

SUMMER

I'm so damn pissed that I can barely unload the plants from the back of my Jeep. Somehow, I do, and I almost feel bad when I slam them down on my steps. Unfortunately, I know this is the last time they'll look this colorful and healthy, so I bend over and smell them, hoping it will clear my mind.

It doesn't.

I unlock the door and walk inside my house, kicking off my shoes. I sit on the small couch, and while I'd usually turn on the TV and mindlessly scroll the channels, I can't. My mind races, and I can't stop replaying the interaction with Beckett.

What the hell is wrong with him? Why would he ask me on a date, of all things?

It's so out of character for him that I feel like he did it to test me. One thing is certain: Beckett Valentine would never give me the time of day. Not his little sister's best friend, the girl he's never treated like a woman.

No, he has to be up to something, and right now, I trust him as far as I can throw him. He's too muscular, too tall, too built, and lifting him off the ground would be impossible. Just as impossible as him legitimately wanting to go on a date with me.

If his goal was to confuse his opponent, he's won. Because I have no idea what to think about any of this, which frustrates me even more. Not only am I constantly at war with myself but I'm at war with him. It's not an easy position to be in. I hate how he can get me so worked up with a sarcastic smile. He's too good-looking for his own good, and that frustrates the piss out of me.

As I'm stewing in my anger, my phone vibrates. I pull my phone from my pocket to see a text from Kinsley.

> Girl! I MANIFESTED A RAISE!

> A raise? Didn't you say you were going to get fired?

> I know, right? We should celebrate tonight. Do you have any plans?

This has me laughing because she knows I don't. If I'm not hanging out with her, I'm at home researching different ways to keep plants alive or studying different bed-and-breakfasts in the state.

> Checked my calendar, looks like it's wide open. For the next five years.

> Meet me at Boot Scooting at 7 pm. All drinks are on me.

Boot Scooting is one of the local country music bars in town that has a nice dance floor and pool tables in the back. They'll have country karaoke a few times per month, or bands will come in and play live music. There's lots of line dancing, too. Kinsley and I have often sat at the bar and drank shots, only to call one of her brothers to pick us up because we couldn't drive home. Fun times. But I'm not searching for a hangover tonight.

I think about it for a few more seconds, and she impatiently sends a text.

????????????

> Okay, okay. I'll meet you there. I'm not drinking a ton, though. Like one drink.

> I'm pretty sure you've told me that every single time we've nearly crawled out of that place.

I snicker because she's right.

> I'll be there, but if I wake up with a massive headache tomorrow, you're coming over to help me feed the animals.

Deal.

Well, that was easy.

I check the time and see it's barely past three, and I've already finished everything that I needed to do today. I could wash a load of clothes or put up the dishes I started before I left this morning, but I decide to nap instead. I need a mental reset.

Three hours pass in a blink, and thankfully, I don't dream about anything. I didn't realize how tired I was. Staying up late the night before and getting up early caught up with me, but at least I feel rested. Getting dressed doesn't take very long, and it's only a ten-minute drive to the bar.

The parking lot is full, which I expected, considering it's a Friday night. It's when most locals go out after a hard week of work. Once I park, I text Kinsley and let her know I'm here. When I see her truck, I climb out of my Jeep and meet her on the sidewalk. She's dressed in short-as-hell shorts, cowboy boots, and a tank top.

I look her up and down. "We're literally almost twinning."

"It's because we're basically the same person. I'm kinda sad I didn't wear a miniskirt now." She loops her arm in mine and leads me inside.

"It's comfy, and who knows, maybe I'll find a date."

Her red lips crack into a smile. "That's the spirit. Oh, I told one of the guys on the datin' app that we'd be here tonight."

My eyes go wide, and I laugh. "That's amazing! Do you think he'll come?"

"I dunno. I hope. He's hot as hell. But I want to ensure you get a good vibe from him, or I'm kicking his ass straight to the curb." We enter the dim room, then walk to the bar. There are a few stools available, so we choose a few at the end.

"So he's the third wheel, right?" I smirk.

"Of course. If he can't hang out with us and make it fun, he has no business tryin' to date me. What's the sayin'? Bros before hos."

I snicker. "And same. I wouldn't know what to do with myself if I ended up with someone you didn't like."

"It'd never happen. You're a picky bitch."

"Total truth bomb."

The bartender greets us with a flirty smile. He's got dark hair and a few tattoos, and his button-up shirt sleeves are rolled to his elbows. I'd probably ask him out if he weren't at least six years younger than me. Younger guys just aren't my thing, not even for a random fling.

He meets Kinsley's eyes and lingers on her for a minute before looking my way.

"What are you two ladies havin' tonight?"

"Somethin' with bite." Kinsley chews on the corner of her lip. "I'm feelin' pretty feisty."

He growls and pops a brow. "What about a Sit On My Face shot?"

Kinsley lifts her brow. "I'll have two, and so will she."

I laugh. "And that's how you end up pregnant."

She pats her arm. "That's why we have implants."

"Touché."

A few minutes pass, and our shots are set down in front of us. Kinsley slides her card across the bar and opens a tab for us. "I'm takin' care of the bill tonight. Anything she orders is on me."

He looks back and forth between us. "Y'all together?"

Kinsley wraps her arm around me. "Not sexually, just emotionally."

I shake my head and look at her when he walks away. "You're gonna give him a hard-on."

She lifts her shot and waits for me to do the same. "To one day becoming a MILF."

I nearly lose it because it was not what I expected her to say. Then again, how could I? Most of what she says comes out of left field.

"To one day becoming a MILF." We *tink* our glasses together and swallow them down. It's sweet, delicious even, but also very dangerous because the alcohol taste is covered by sugar.

"These will get us into trouble." I grab the other and lift it. "To your raise and one day you running that damn newspaper."

"Hear, hear." Kinsley grins wide, and we swallow the second shot in one big gulp.

The bartender comes back around and picks up the empty shot glasses, and Kinsley ups her flirting game. "We want more shots."

"Yeah? Whatcha in the mood for?"

She looks at him from head to toe. "A few strong *Screaming Orgasms.*"

"Mm. I'd love to help make that happen." He studies her for a second, then walks away.

"Is he flirting with me?" She turns to me when we're alone. "Or am I just imagining we have a connection goin'?"

I snort. "Might be the Sit On My Faces. Also, did you make that drink up?"

"No. It's real. I have all the dirty-as-hell drink names memorized. Blow Job. Creamy Pussy. Death by Sex. Shall I keep goin'?"

I can't stop laughing, and it's not because of the two shots. It's because Kinsley is something else. "Sure, can you name four more?"

"Piece of cake." She counts on her fingers. "Leg Spreader, Sex on the Beach, Muff Diver, and one of my favorites, a Porn Star martini. I can seriously do this *all* night."

"You're a pro. What can I say?"

"Two Screaming Orgasms." The bartender sets two creamy-looking martinis in front of us, and I hope it tastes better than it looks.

Kinsley leans forward. "Oh, hey, what's your name?"

"Luca."

"You're not from 'round here." Kinsley beams.

"Nah, I'm new in town. Only been here about a month. Diana Dalhart is my mom's sister. I'm staying for the summer."

"And then what're ya gonna do?" Kinsley blinks up at him. Her long eyelashes flutter as she twirls the stirring straws in her Screaming Orgasm.

He shrugs. "Depends. Might stick around. Might move back to New York."

"Ahh, New York. A city slicker." Kinsley grins. Her flirting game is on point.

"No, I grew up in Texas. Just in New York to make connections 'cause I'm a musician."

"Oh, nice." Kinsley seems impressed. Someone calls for Luca, and he excuses himself.

I meet Kinsley's eyes. "Don't you dare go home with him. This is how heartbreak begins. Plus, haven't you learned anything from the internet? Never trust a musician."

"I'm not lookin' for love. So if my e-man doesn't show, at

least I'll have someone else to occupy me tonight." She winks, and I know she's not kidding.

"Your famous last words." I chuckle as her eyes widen, and she shifts in front of me.

"Shit." She looks annoyed.

"Did the online guy just walk in?" I try to catch a glimpse, but she keeps my attention and tries to hide in front of me.

"Stay still," she says, positioning herself forward, covering her face with her hand. I don't understand why she's acting this way, considering she set up the meeting with this guy.

"Fancy seein' you here," I hear from behind me. My entire body tingles when I hear his voice, and I know exactly who's here. Her brother. Beckett motherfucking Valentine.

I glare at him, sucking in a deep breath. "You're like a cockroach that won't go away."

"Then you must be trash I like meddling in." He slaps my insult right back.

Kinsley looks at me apologetically and then glares at him. "We're having a girls' night."

"And I'm having a beer." He sits on the empty stool next to me.

"That seat is taken." My nostrils flare.

"It sure is. Taken by me." He tries to get the bartender's attention.

"No. I don't want you to sit by me."

He looks at me, peering into my soul with his deep sea-blue eyes. "Tough titty."

As soon as Luca returns, Beckett orders a Budweiser. I turn my body toward Kinsley, where my back faces Beckett. "What were we talking about before we were rudely interrupted?"

"Rudely? Whatever."

His mere presence annoys me. And I wish I didn't think the fresh scent of his cologne mixed with his soap smelled good.

"Well, you weren't invited." Kinsley speaks directly to him, and I know they're in one of those brother-sister stare-down battles they always have.

"Last time I checked, this was a public place, and I didn't have to be invited to walk in and order a beer from Luca here." He grabs his frosted mug and pulls it close to him. "So sorry to inconvenience you. If you don't want me around, go somewhere and drink your cum drinks." He gives my martini glass a glance before meeting my eyes.

I try hard to ignore him, and I'm about eight seconds from telling Kinsley that I need to leave. But because we're celebrating her, I don't.

Kinsley huffs and snatches her martini glass, then chugs it down. I decide to do the same, and I'm surprised by how delicious it tastes.

She meets my gaze. "You want another Screaming O?"

Beckett shakes his head, then lifts the beer to his perfect lips and takes a big drink.

He's insufferably sexy without even trying, and I hate how my body responds to his closeness. Not to mention he's wearing a black T-shirt that shows his full sleeve of tattoos. I'm doomed. I'm fucking doomed.

At eight o'clock, the lights dim, and the dancing music begins. A crowd forms, and when Beckett reaches forward to grab his second beer, his arm brushes against mine. Just the touch of him causes an inferno to rage inside me. My breath quickens, and Beckett leans over and whispers in my ear.

"So about that date?"

"Absolutely not." My heart won't stop fluttering.

The bastard chuckles, and when Luca comes over and asks me if I want to order another drink, I'm relieved.

"A martini, extra dirty."

"Just how I like it." Beckett takes a drink.

Kinsley leans in and speaks so only I can hear her. "He's here."

I look over my shoulder and see a tall guy wearing a nice cowboy hat and a plaid button-up shirt.

"That's him?" I meet her gaze.

"Who?" Beckett butts in.

"Nonya." Kinsley glares at him.

Beckett turns around and spots the guy. "That pud? What about him?"

"Shut up." Kinsley wags her finger at her brother, then waves in the man's direction. I kind of have to agree with Beckett on this one, which pains me.

Kinsley puts on her sexiest smile, and when he's closer, she wraps her arms around his neck and gives him a hug. "Jude, you made it!"

"Of course I did." He lifts her and spins her around. When Kinsley is back on her feet, she moves closer to me. "This is my best friend, Summer."

"Hi, Summer. It's nice to meet you. Kinsley's told me a lot about you."

"All good things, I hope."

Beckett chuckles, then twists around in his stool, holding his beer. "I'm Beckett. Kinsley's older brother."

He's intimidating and could smoosh this guy under his boot.

"Nice to meet you." Jude shakes Beckett's hand. Immediately, I know it was a mistake.

When they release their grasp, Jude shakes out his hand, and I know Beckett was a complete dick and nearly crushed his fingers.

Jude meets Kinsley's eyes. "Didn't realize it would be a family affair."

"Trust me, I didn't either." She sucks in a deep breath, and Beckett acts completely unfazed by Jude's comment. He plays the dickhead older brother part well. Lots of years of practice, I suppose.

My martini is delivered, and I sip it. Jude and Kinsley chat, and that leaves me with my drink. Honestly, I'd rather talk to myself than try to hold a conversation with Beckett. Soon, a woman squeezes herself between me and him to get the bartender's attention.

"'Scuse me." She leans into him. "Sorry, didn't mean to get so close."

I roll my eyes.

"Hey, it's fine. Not an inconvenience to have a pretty lady near me."

"Mm. You single?"

"For now." They laugh together.

Heat rushes to my cheeks, and I take a big gulp of my drink, wanting to disappear.

Kinsley turns to me. "You okay?"

"Gonna go to the bathroom real quick." I excuse myself, and the woman slides onto my stool. It's official, I'm having the worst time I could've ever imagined.

As I make my way across the dance floor, I realize how much I've drunk, because the world tilts on its axis. I laugh, realizing Kinsley was right, and I've gone and done exactly what I said I wouldn't—have more than one drink.

The ladies' restroom is apparently a hip place to be, because there's a line in the hallway, and I'm at the end. I have to wait outside for a good ten minutes before I'm finally let in. My bladder is so full that I nearly burst when I'm able to do my business. Sweet relief. As I wash my hands, I look in the mirror at myself. Women move in and out, and pretty soon, I'm alone.

I take my time, not wanting to go back out there and hear Beckett openly flirting with some stranger. Who knows, she's probably already made herself more than comfortable in my seat. Something he'd probably prefer. When I finally walk out, I find Beckett leaning against the wall with his hands in his pockets, waiting.

I glare at him. "What are you doin'?"

He grabs my hand and pulls me toward him. "Makin' sure you're okay."

"Don't. I don't need you lookin' out for me."

I think back to that unforgettable night at senior prom. I was just a freshman, and I'd wished on all the falling stars that Beckett would ask me to be his date. The flirting between us was unfathomable, and while I knew he was older, it didn't matter to me. However, I waited around, and he ended up getting asked by someone else and said yes. Then another guy his age asked me, so I took the opportunity to attend. Not many freshmen were invited to go, not even Kinsley, and she was always Miss Popular.

We learned later it was because Beckett threatened to rip off anyone's dick who even glanced at his little sister the wrong way. But me?

I was fair game. And that night, I played the part of a pawn.

I'm brought back to reality when Beckett lifts my chin with his finger and forces me to look up into his crystal-blue eyes. I feel as if I'm floating in this dim hallway.

"Why you gotta be so damn stubborn?" His low and husky voice causes goose bumps to trail up my arms when his warm breath brushes against my cheeks.

"Isn't that your middle name?" I counter.

He gives me a smug look.

"Where'd your woman for the night go?" I'm nearly breathless as my heart hammers in my chest. He's too close.

Beckett leans in, and his lips brush against my ear. "Right in front of me."

"You're drunk. Or stupid. Maybe even both."

He chuckles. "Not quite, SumSum."

"Stop it. Tell me your bid." I back up, creating space between us before I do something I regret.

"You know the rules." His brows are raised. "But I'll make another deal with you."

"Listening."

"One round of pool. You win, I tell you my number. You lose, you go on a date with me, then I'll still tell you my number."

"Seems to me I win either way."

He shrugs. "Guess it depends on how you look at it."

I hold out my hand, and we shake on it. "That's a deal."

When he smirks, I feel as if I'm dying. "Great. You lead the way."

Beckett holds out his hand, and I walk past him.

He knows my daddy taught me how to play, and I can shoot with the best. Tonight is the night Beckett will finally go down, and I couldn't be more excited.

12

BECKETT

S ummer is cocky as hell, always has been, and I know she thinks she has a chance at beating me. Sure, I know her dad taught her how to play, and she's good, but she's not better than me. She was pretty confident back in the hallway, thinking she already won.

A cheeky grin touches my lips as I follow her to the pool room.

She's wearing a skirt so damn short that I can see the bottom of her ass cheeks from certain angles. It's an image that will be imprinted in my mind for years to come.

All the pool tables are full, so Summer barges in and announces she's next. When their beady eyes slide up and down her body, I take a step forward with my arms crossed. They quickly get the hint to back the fuck off.

"You want another drink?" I meet her gaze.

"Tryin' to get me drunk so you'll have an advantage?"

I shrug. "Fine then. I'll be back. At least try not to get into any trouble while I'm away." I walk to the bar and grab another beer. I find Kinsley still sitting with this dude wearing a cowboy costume.

"Where's Summer?" She looks around.

"We're 'bout to play a round of pool." I wave down Luca, who nods.

"You are?" She looks puzzled.

"Yeah. Don't act so shocked."

Her mouth is still open, and she closes it, then narrows her eyes. "You're up to somethin'."

"Nah. If you need us, we'll be in the back."

I point to where Summer is, and Kinsley stands up and waves at her. Summer waves back. After I grab my beer, I head back to her. I enter the room and stand beside her, watching the current game.

"Almost time for you to lose for good."

She's already started shit-talking. This should be great.

"Lose? Sweetheart, I win either fuckin' way you look at it." I'll get to spend time with her for the next thirty minutes, or we'll go on a date. The way I see it, I've already won.

She shakes her head. "Too cocky for your own good."

"Like the kettle callin' the pot black." One of the guys sinks the eight ball in the far left pocket and wins the game.

I push a few dollars into the change machine, then shove the quarters into the pool machine slot so it will release the balls. They flood out, and Summer grabs the triangle, then sets the table as I rub chalk on the end of my cue stick.

On the radio, Reba McEntire plays, and it's the perfect soundtrack.

"You wanna break?"

With a mischievous grin, she lifts her brows, and moves toward the table.

It's a risky game I'm playing. Years ago, I watched her win five hundred dollars in cash from dudes talking shit. She smeared their faces in defeat. It was interesting to see her win without apology.

Summer sets her stick, bending over, giving me the perfect view of her sweet ass, then pulls back and cracks the cue ball into the others. Stripes and solids spread along the felt of the table, and two solids drop into the side pockets.

"We're calling shots." I'm not going easy on her because if I give her an inch, she will take a damn mile.

"Didn't expect anything less." She bends over. "Middle right." In goes the two ball. "Far left."

The guys who had the table before us watch the game, and pretty soon, a small crowd forms.

"Don't get too cocky now."

She walks by, brushing against me, and the smell of her shampoo and body wash surrounds me. "Cocky? Ha. It's called being confident in my skills. Middle left."

She makes it, leaving three more solids and the eight ball. I've not had the opportunity to shoot once, and I just hope she gets too in her head and misses. Just one chance, that's all I need.

More people surround us, and they ooh and aah. If I didn't know better, I'd say she's getting a kick out of the attention, especially considering she hasn't missed one *yet*. I stand at the head of the table, keeping my focus on her. Her eyes dart around as she tries to figure out her next move.

When she's deep in thought, she tugs on the corner of her plump lips. As if she notices me staring, she looks up at me with big green eyes. Her lips slightly part before she stands straight and walks past me.

"'Scuse me." Summer stands right in front of me and then bends over. My eyes trail down her back to her cute little waist, and I focus on her ass before stepping back. She's such a cock tease.

"Four ball, middle left." She takes her sweet time.

"Impossible." I shove one hand into my pocket.

She glances at me over her shoulder, repositions her body, then goes for it.

Everyone waits with bated breath as the cue ball hits the

side of another and then smacks into the four, but it doesn't have enough force to sink it.

"Told ya so!" I burst into laughter, not trying to rub her nose in it but knowing I have a lot to go without making a mistake. She's nearly cleared the table, making it much easier for me to navigate.

She groans loudly and moves out of the way.

I easily sink three balls into the called pockets.

Kinsley walks up and looks at the table. "Shit."

She sees I'm about to shoot, then turns to look at Summer. "Explain yourself."

Walking past them, trying to get the best angle of approach, I hear Summer tell her about our bet.

Kinsley shakes her head. "You never make deals with the devil. Have I not taught you anything?"

I speak up as I pull my stick back and shoot. "She's right."

Another ball drops into the far left corner.

Summer watches me intensely, the electricity buzzing between us, and if she weren't so stubborn, we wouldn't be doing this in such a public fashion.

"Now, we're tied. Miss this one, and you're done, Valentine."

I shake my head. "All bark and no bite. Middle left. And way too easy." It falls right in. As I walk past her again, I lean in to whisper in her ear. "And you doubted me."

"You two should just get a room already, damn." Kinsley takes a sip of her drink.

"And you should stop drinkin'." I look at her martini, which looks like liquid splooge, then make a face at her. "Let me guess…that a Cum Guzzler?"

She snorts and shrugs. I have a feeling I'll be driving her home tonight if she keeps this up.

I glance at Summer. "So where do you want to go? A dinner date?"

The death glare I receive honestly brings me too much joy. "It's not over yet."

I call my shot. The cue ball strikes against the one I need, which hits the side wall, then falls into the hole. When I glance over my shoulder at her, she swallows hard.

Kinsley looks between us and shakes her head.

"Two balls." I chuckle.

She rolls her eyes. "Should kiss yours goodbye if you force me to go out with you."

I let out a howl of laughter. "Fiesty. My favorite."

"I think I just threw up in my mouth." Summer pretends to barf as I sink another ball.

All that's left on the table is one stripe and the eight. Summer's eyes are wide as she watches the scene unfold. As I bend over to strike my second-to-last ball, I feel a hand on my cock. Summer's wearing a devilish grin as she gently squeezes my balls. Her touch has me instantly growing hard.

"Playin' dirty, I see. Go ahead. Get a good handful so you can find out what your workin' with."

Her face turns beet red.

I lower my voice and smirk. "Nothin' you can do will distract me, SumSum. Grab my dick all you want. Touch my ass. Feel me up, baby. Only encourages me to beat that ass."

Kinsley lets out a roar of laughter. "He's immune to that shit."

Summer huffs and crosses her arms over her chest.

"Guess you're done, then?"

She rolls her eyes.

"Let's go ahead and get this over with, shall we?" My final ball hits the edge of the eight, slamming it to the side, and for a moment, I'm scared it might slide into the hole, which would make this game over. Thankfully, it doesn't, and my stripe does. Now I'm perfectly set up to win, and I try my damnedest not to gloat.

Summer's grin fades to a scowl. "This is bullshit."

"Warned ya not to get too cocky."

"Now, time for me to finish this up so we can plan that date. Eight ball, far right." My heart thumps hard in my chest as I powder my hands. I can't fuck this up, not now, not when I'm so close to having the chance of a lifetime.

"Any last words?" I meet Summer's gaze as I bend over and get into position.

"I hope you miss." Her breasts are rising and falling with each passing second. The people around the pool table quiet down, and all that can be heard is the overhead music and laughter coming from the bar.

The pressure is intense. And I bet she's hoping I lose so she can mop the table. Unfortunately for her, I don't plan on missing.

I clear my throat, pull the stick back, then watch as it connects with the white ball that crashes into the eight. It zooms across the opposite side of the table and slides right into the pocket I called.

The room bursts into applause, and everyone is smiling—everyone except Summer.

I put my stick into the holder.

"Best two out of three?" She raises her eyebrows as if I'd go for that.

I shake my head. "A deal is a deal."

"Damn." Kinsley pats her on the back. "At least you tried."

Summer closes her eyes tight. "Ugh. I'm so pissed at myself for taking the bait."

"What is it you said earlier about confidence?" I lift a brow, and her eyes bolt open.

"Hush. So when do I have to make good on this stupid bet?"

"Tomorrow night."

"No. I…I…"

"You got plans?" I already know the answer.

"No, but I need time to prepare."

"Tomorrow night." I stand firm. "I'll pick you up at your place at seven."

"But..."

"No takebacks. Seven on the dot. Wear something..." I look at her from head to toe. "You can get dirty in."

Summer looks like she wants to murder me, and I'm okay with that.

"What does that even mean?" Kinsley turns her head toward me.

"Don't worry about it, sis. Also, where's your lame date?"

"Oh, he had to leave. Had to drive home before it got too late."

I check the time on my phone. "It's ten."

She shrugs. "He has to be up early for work."

"You gonna date him?"

Her eyes go wide. "That's none of your damn business, now, is it? Pretty sure I'm nearly thirty and can date and fuck whoever I want."

"True, but pretty sure I'm your older brother, and I can fuck up anyone you date if they treat you poorly."

Kinsley holds out her hand as if she's presenting something. "And this, ladies and gentlemen, is why I will be single for the rest of my life."

"So what's my excuse?" Summer laughs.

"And this is why she will be single, too."

Summer playfully smacks her arm. "Doubt he's cockblocking me...still."

There's only one dude who I cockblocked from Summer. The night of prom. And neither of us has forgotten it.

If I'd not shown up when I did, she would've been taken advantage of by Daniel Davis. He'd bragged after school one day that he was going to take Summer Jones's virginity the night of our senior prom. From that point on, it was my mission to protect her from assholes like him. And when the time came at the after-party when he led Summer up the stairs, I followed them.

He'd given her too much to drink, and I saw she wasn't in the right state of mind. She was too sweet, too pretty to have her virginity ripped away without full consent. When he brought her into the room, I burst inside as he was unzipping his pants. Summer was barely able to keep her eyes open. That night, I beat the fuck out of Daniel without any regrets. And I'd do it one hundred times over to save her from that asshole.

It spread around town, and by Monday, everyone at school knew what had happened. However, ever since that moment, we've been at each other's throats. Maybe it wasn't my place to step in, but I didn't care. I was protecting her, and even now, I'd kick anyone's ass for trying to take advantage of her.

Summer has always said I've treated her like my little sister, but she's just too naive to realize it's much more than that. Always has been.

She meets my eyes. "Why do you have that look on your face?"

I immediately smile. "Just thinkin' about things. See you tomorrow."

She lets out a growl as I turn to Kinsley. "You need a ride home?"

Summer shakes her head. "I'll take her."

"Are you good to drive?" I meet her eyes.

Kinsley loops her arms in Summer's. "We're *not* ready to leave yet."

Summer shrugs. "I'll be fine."

I suck in a deep breath, deciding that I'll stay until they leave just to make sure they're okay. There's no way in hell I'm leaving them here alone on a Friday night. There are too many wandering eyeballs.

Kinsley and Summer go onto the dance floor. They two-step with each other, and every dude in the place nearly salivates. I make my way back to the bar, find a stool, and order water. At this point, I'm convinced they're gonna close this place down tonight. Not something I planned on either.

I just wanted to grab a quick beer, people watch for a bit, then go home. Just as I take my first sip, I see some douchebag walk up to my sister and Summer. He's trying to butt in, and I can see Kinsley shaking her head.

I'm trying my damnedest to stay out of it, to let them handle themselves, but the moment he grabs Summer's arms, I see fucking red. Slamming my water onto the bar top, I get up and march across the dance floor.

"You got a fuckin' problem?" I tower over the asshole.

He looks up at me, and I swear his eyes blink separately, but then he pushes me out of the way.

"Fuck off, they're mine."

I barely budge. Sucking in a deep breath, I try to calm myself so I don't knock this guy into next year and go to jail tonight.

"Don't." Summer places her hand softly on my chest, stepping between us. A small crowd of locals forms, but the room is mostly full of college students from the town over.

The drunk guy stumbles. "That's what I thought."

Summer shakes her head. "He's not worth it, Beck."

When she uses my nickname, I peer into her eyes. "Okay." She doesn't take her gaze from mine. "Okay," I repeat.

Meanwhile, Kinsley is busy running her mouth, yelling for the bouncer to kick this asshole out. Soon, a big guy named Bull walks up, takes the pipsqueak by his shirt collar, and drags him away.

Summer takes a step back, creating space between us, breaking the energetic charge.

Kinsley grabs Summer's hands as if nothing happened. "Now, back to dancing."

They boot scoot with the rest of the crowd. I go back to the bar, adrenaline and anger still pumping through me. The audacity. If I ever see that punk on the street, I'll give him a shiner for disrespecting them. Sometimes, guys like that need to learn a hard lesson about treating ladies with respect. I crack my knuckles, trying to calm myself, but don't take my eyes off them. Kinsley keeps drinking, but Summer hasn't had another drop since I arrived. I open my phone, see a missed text from Harrison, and I shake my head when I read it.

> Can you feed the horses tomorrow evenin'?

> Got a date planned tomorrow night.

> Omg. With who? Poor girl.

I chuckle.

> I don't think I'm gonna tell ya. But the answer is no.

> But I have a date tomorrow night, too!

> Better text someone else, bro. I got plans.

> You never have plans. What are the odds?

> It was a one-in-a-million shot. Good luck findin' someone, bud.

I don't send another text and shove my phone back into my pocket. I'd be happy to cover for him if I didn't have plans, and I've done it a handful of times since we've been training together. But tomorrow is a hard no.

When I look up, Summer and Kinsley are heading toward me.

"I think we're ready to go." Kinsley's slurring as she points her finger into my chest. "You're driving me home."

"Why the change of heart?" I search her face.

"She puked," Summer says. "I can drive myself home."

"I'm followin' you the whole way."

She cashes out Kinsley's tab for her, then helps her outside.

I meet them at my truck, noticing my sister is three sheets to the wind.

"Shoulda slowed down on your cum shots." I chuckle as Summer buckles her in and shuts the door. I roll the passenger window down. "Where're ya parked?"

"Just over there." That's when I see her bright yellow Jeep. I nod, and she makes her way there, her ass shaking with each step. When she gets inside and turns on the lights, I pull up behind her, giving her enough space to reverse. She leads the way home.

"So you're finally goin' on a date with Summer." Kinsley laughs with her eyes closed. I left the window down just in case she decides to throw up. At least then, she can lean her head out.

"And what's funny about it?" I glance over at her.

"I'm glad, honestly. You two have been needin' to hate-fuck each other out of your systems for years."

I smirk. "There is no hate-fuckin' happenin', Kins. I want her to have a good time."

Her eyes bolt open, and she points at me. "And that's exactly why some kinda fuckin' is in the future. Summer's never had a proper date, never been out with a perfect gentleman. Don't fuck this up, Beckett. Or I'll make sure to chop your dick off."

"Like I'm scared."

"You should be." She waves her finger. "Ya know, I'm still holdin' on to hope that you'll both stop bein' so stubborn and finally see how much alike you are."

This makes me smile. We are a lot alike, more than either of us has ever wanted to admit. Kinsley calls it stubborn. I call it passionate. There's a difference.

"We'll see."

"She likes you. Like a lot."

"She said that?" I like that her inhibitions are down. Although I'm sure Summer wouldn't.

"No, she'd never admit it. But I've seen the way she looks at you. The way she's *always* looked at you."

I don't say anything.

"It's the same way you look at her."

Summer's blinker clicks on, and she slows, then turns into the driveway that leads to her small cabin, the same road I'll take tomorrow to pick her up. I pass the Horseshoe Creek Ranch, then turn onto my parents' property and drive the short distance to where Kinsley lives. She had it built a few years ago with money she saved from the newspaper.

I park and then look at her. "Ya need me to walk ya in?"

She shakes her head. "No, but I'll need ya to help me get my truck tomorrow."

"Depends on what time you roll out of bed."

She shrugs. "I'll text you. Oh, and Summer's favorite dessert is chocolate cake."

"I know."

She looks almost puzzled. "You do?"

"Kins, I know what she likes and doesn't like. I know she kills flowers like the grim reaper, and when she's lying or deep in thought, the side of her lip slightly tilts up."

She meets my eyes. "You're so getting married. I'm manifesting it."

I shake my head. "You and that woo stuff."

"I seriously can't wait to tell you *I told you so*."

"Yeah? And I can't wait for you to get back together with Hayden so I can say the same to you."

Her eyes go wide, and I swear if she hadn't drunk so much, she'd have clocked me between the eyes. We've been told to pretend he doesn't exist, and she's dead set on keeping it that way, but I bring him up every chance I get because they were made for each other.

"Yep. You're still an asshole." She opens the door and hops

out, nearly stumbling. "The asshole who's going to make my bestie my sister."

"Whatever you say!" I yell.

She walks the short distance to her porch, laughing.

Honestly, I hope she's right. I'd happily take that *I told you so* on the chin.

I wait for her to go inside the house before reversing and heading to my place on the other side of the property.

Tomorrow, I have a date with the woman I've dreamed of taking out since I was seventeen. The pressure is on. And if it weren't for the Horseshoe Creek Ranch going up for sale, I'm not sure this opportunity would've ever arisen. But then again, as Kinsley says, what should happen, will happen. Maybe she's right.

13

SUMMER

I've been a nervous wreck all morning. I fed the horses, saw my parents, called Kinsley, and texted her about a million times. I'm trying to play it cool, pretending I've never wanted to date Beckett, but it's a lie.

As I'm walking into the grocery store to pick up some more coffee, I spot Beckett. My heart races, and I stop and watch him from the opposite end of the aisle. There's no way he spotted me, because he's too busy studying the different flours. Off to his side, Mrs. Petree is standing on her tiptoes, trying to grab some vegetable oil that's just out of her reach.

He gives her his million-dollar grin, then walks over and easily swipes it off the top shelf. He's wearing a T-shirt that hugs his body, displaying all the hard muscle lines he's covering.

"You puttin' all this up in your car alone?" Beckett swipes his hand through his hair.

"My grandson couldn't come with me today. Had baseball practice."

"I'll help you. How much longer ya gonna be?"

Mrs. Petree smiles wide. "About twenty minutes. Meet me up front?"

"Yes, ma'am. I'll be there."

I swallow hard, rushing to grab a can of coffee grounds. I practically jog to the front of the store, wishing we had things like self-checkout so I can escape before running into him. After a few minutes, I look around and check my phone. Mr. Delano takes his time writing a check, and I'm ready to explode with impatience.

"Gettin' ready for our date?" Beckett's deep voice tickles my spine as his warm breath brushes against my neck.

I don't move. I don't think I can handle looking into his eyes right now. "Nope. Ain't got nothin' to prepare for."

He chuckles. "Whatever you say, SumSum. Gonna make it worth your while."

Mrs. Petree stands in the other line and waves at Beckett. She points to the front windows. "I'm parked right there."

"I'll be there."

I finally turn to face him. "That's kind of you to help her."

He shrugs. "It's nothin'. I'd want someone to help my Mawmaw, too."

I give him a smile, then I turn my back to him when the cashier scans my coffee and gives my total.

"Seven on the dot," he reminds me as I'm handed my bag.

I playfully roll my eyes at him, then walk to my Jeep with my heart fluttering. The Beckett I saw in there is the person I crushed on all those years ago before he proved to me how much of a shithead he can be.

As I make my way home, I can't stop thinking about last night. When that guy grabbed my arm, rage overtook Beckett. The creep was drunk, being overly pushy, but Kinsley was handling him just fine. Beckett possessively walked over, and I caught a glimpse of the same protective look I saw all those years ago.

I didn't want him to get kicked out or arrested for fighting, so I tried to calm him down.

When I peered into his blue eyes, I saw the real him. The one he hides from me and everyone else. There are times when

I see the person inside him that I crushed on all those years ago, the Beckett that's kind and protective. In the grocery store, I was reminded that that man still exists, and at times, it's hard to hate him.

On the way home, I feel lost in a mixture of emotions.

I have no idea what to wear or how to act, or what even to expect.

For the rest of the day, I organize some paperwork Dad needed help with. We've been selling a lot of livestock lately, so I'll go into the business account a few times a month and file things away. Dad is comfortable in the saddle but not behind a computer.

I busy myself for hours, and when I finally pull away from my laptop, I realize Beckett will be at my house in less than two hours to pick me up. I need to get dressed, but it feels like a prank, a setup to let me crash and burn. Maybe he needs the confirmation that he'd never date me, a girl he thinks of like a sister. I suppose I expect that, considering we've grown up together.

My phone buzzes on the counter as I make a glass of sweet tea.

I pick it up and see it's Kinsley.

"What are you wearing tonight?" She sounds way too excited.

"Can you hear my thoughts or something?" I chuckle.

"No, but I kinda wish I could so then I'd know what you truly think about Beckett."

"Please. Don't be dramatic. You're not missing much."

No matter how much I deny my feelings about him, she doesn't believe it. She never has and never will. The last thing I want to do is admit it and get my hopes up or be let down. I'd rather never give him a chance than be rejected. It's easier that way. Or at least that's what I tell myself.

"Do you have any idea what he has planned?" I wonder if she was able to get him to talk.

"I wish. I begged him to tell me when he brought me to town to get my truck this morning. He refused. Said I have a big mouth."

This makes me laugh. "Well, I mean, he *is* kinda right."

"I wouldn't have told you!" Now she's trying to convince me of something I know isn't true.

"Lies. You would've given me a hint or something. Right now, I don't know what to think. Do I dress in heels? Do I dress in shorts? Maybe I should wait until he shows up to see what he's wearing before I decide what to put on. Ugh. I hate surprises!" I grab my tea and plop down on the couch. "And time is ticking."

"I'm going to text him and see if he'll at least tell me what you need to wear. How 'bout that?"

"Oh, that would be awesome *if* he'd be nice and tell you for once."

"Hold on. I'll message him now."

I can hear the blip sounds of text.

"Sent."

"I wish I wouldn't have made that stupid bet. I've been anxious about this since last night. I could barely sleep."

"It's going to be fine. One date, then you'll know his bid and can do your thang. Just remember, it's just one step closer to winning."

"You're right." I almost forgot that was the point of this. I've been so wrapped up in being alone with Beckett that the most important reason I'm doing this slipped my mind.

"Oh, just got a text back." She goes silent for a moment. "It was unhelpful."

"Do I even want to know what he said?"

She sighs. "Nope. No, you don't."

"Great." I groan. "Fine. I'm wearing the first thing I pull out of my dresser."

Kinsley chuckles. "He kinda deserves that after saying clothes are optional."

"I honestly expected nothing less. Seems like something he'd say. Well, I have an hour to figure it out. Guess tonight is going to be a choose-your-own-adventure."

"You still got your bridesmaid dress from your parents' marriage renewal?" Kinsley barely gets the words out between her laughter.

"Uh, yeah. Hangin' in the back of my closet, collectin' dust. Shit. That's a good idea."

"I'm not saying you should wear it, but it would be quite hilarious."

"You're a bad influence, ya know."

I can tell she's smiling when she speaks. "Oh, I'm well aware. I just like to give Beckett a run for his money. It's not often any of us get the opportunity."

"I'm gonna think about it. My luck, he'll take me frog huntin' or somethin'. The last thing I want to do is be out by the old pond in a formal dress."

"Didn't think about that. Yeah, ya better play it safe for your sake. Don't want it to backfire on you."

We both know she's right, because Beckett is unpredictable.

"Not gonna take my chances. Jeans and a T-shirt with a hoodie it is. He told me to wear somethin' I can get dirty in, but I don't believe him. Guess he'll get the old usual me."

"You'll have to let me know where he takes you. He was super secretive about it. He wouldn't even tell Harrison."

"Oh great, the whole family knows this is happening?"

She chuckles. "Yeah, they all know. Even my parents."

"How is that possible?"

"Harrison texted our family group chat and told everyone Beckett was going on a date. Then he asked us to help him with his horse feedin' chores. He told them it was because big bro was going on a date…with *you*. I'll spare you what everyone said, but they gave Beckett a very hard time."

My cheeks heat. I had hoped it would be something that we did and no one knew about—

well, no one other than Kinsley. The next thing I know, my parents will know, too. "I'm going to kill Harrison."

"Be my guest. He needs a good ass-kickin'."

I look at the time on my phone. "Guess I should let you go so I can get ready. I'll fill you in on all the details."

"You can leave out the sex deets."

I gasp. "I'm not fuckin' your brother!"

"I wouldn't blame you if you did."

"Jesus. Hangin' up now!"

"Buh-bye!" she sing-songs before I end the call.

I lean my head against the back of the sofa and stare up at the white ceiling. Needing to clear my mind, I take a quick shower, dry my hair, then slip on some nice jeans, my boots, and a button-up shirt that snatches at the waist. Maybe this will be good enough, and if he shows up wearing a suit or something, I'll put on the formal dress.

By the time I look at my phone again, there are five minutes left. Needing a bit of liquid courage, I pull the bottle of whiskey from my freezer and take two shots. It's so cold, and I breathe out the alcohol. At least I'll be loose.

At seven o'clock, there's a knock on my door, and when I open it, Beckett's standing there, smelling so damn good, holding a bouquet of roses. Yellow ones. My favorite. But there's no way he could know that. Right?

He's wearing a nice pair of jeans, boots, a red button-up shirt, and a jacket. His hair is a mess, and the scruff on his face looks so damn good. I bring my attention down to the roses.

"Flowers?" I take them from him and inhale their sweet scent.

He shoots me his boyish grin. "It's a date, Summer. Isn't that what guys do?"

I laugh. "You're the first."

"Sorry bastards."

I look around outside, but I don't see his truck. "How'd you get here?"

He points at the Appaloosa horse saddled and tied to a tree in the distance. My mouth falls open.

"We're goin' ridin'?"

A smile meets his lips. "You'll see."

I look at him like he's lost his mind. "Uh, okay. Let me put these up. You can come in."

I open the door and step to the side. Beckett enters, and I think it's the first time he's been over since the place was complete. He stands off to the side, watching me pull a vase from under the sink, fill it with water, and then dip the flowers inside.

"You should put the package of stuff in there."

"Huh?" I glance at him.

"There's a package of what Mama has always said is aspirin. You put it in the water, and it keeps them fresh longer." He chuckles. "Please tell me you knew that."

I shake my head. "Nope, probably why the ones I bought myself died after a few days." I unwrap the roses and find the packet, then pour it inside.

"That, or it's because you've got the touch of death. Those plants on your porch have seen better days."

It takes everything I have to hold back my smile. "At least I'm tryin'."

"That's true. You're tryin' as the plants are dyin'."

I let out a breath. "Guess we should get this over with."

He laughs. "Don't be too scared about havin' a good time."

"You're so cocky. What if I have a horrible time?"

"Well, I guess you'll have to let me take you out again to make it up to ya."

I burst into laughter. "Nuh-uh. Not happening. You get one shot, Beckett. Hopefully, it's worth my while. Considering Harrison told the entire town we're goin' out, your datin' reputation is on the line." I walk past him, grabbing my jacket from the closet that's close to the door.

"I'm gonna kick his ass." Beckett mumbles something under his breath as he makes his way to the door. I follow him.

We step off the porch, and I glance at my plants, which don't look *that* bad. I've seen much worst.

"Wait, you only brought one horse?" I meet his eyes. "Do I need to go saddle one up?"

"Nope. And don't worry, I'll ride bitch. Pebbles is great. You'll like her." He unties the reins, steps into the stirrup, then positions himself behind the saddle. My nerves immediately get the best of me, and I swallow hard.

"Come on, I don't bite."

"Yes, you do."

With a chuckle, Beckett waves me over. At this moment, I wonder if I should just turn around and go back inside and tell him to have a good night. I haven't ridden with someone behind me since Kinsley and I were kids stealing ponies in the pasture and riding them bareback.

"A deal is a deal." It's like he can read my mind.

"Fine," I huff. After placing my foot in the stirrup, I slide my leg over the saddle and settle in. Beckett moves forward a bit, and I can feel his hot breath on the back of my neck. He reaches around, grabs the leather reins, and turns the horse toward the driveway.

My hips move in the rhythm of the horse, and my heart races with anticipation.

"You're tense."

Beckett's low gruff has me swallowing hard.

"I'm just here for the ride." Being this close to him makes me breathless.

He hums. "Like the thought of that."

His arm brushes against mine as he guides us to his family's property and down one of the old trails behind the main barn. The sun sets in the distance, and bright oranges and pinks fill the sky.

"It's golden hour." Everything is splashed in warm color.

"Yeah, it is. My favorite time of day, either morning or evening."

"Me too." I smile as we mosey down the trail.

It's so quiet I can hear the light breeze blowing through the grasses and trees. Crickets chirp, a sure sign that summer months are right around the corner. The horse's hooves pound against the ground, and I try to take in the moment as Beckett's cologne surrounds me.

Fifteen minutes later, we make it to the end of the trail that leads to the pond we used to toss rocks across as kids. A table and chairs are set up, along with a picnic basket and a bottle of wine. The firepit has a stack of wood with an oversized blanket on the ground.

He brings Pebbles to a stop, slides off, then holds out his hand to help me down. I allow it and nearly fall into his chest.

"I've got you," he mutters, and I meet his gaze.

An inferno rushes through me, and I try to put it out, but it's no use.

Beckett brings Pebbles to the water trough off to the side, then ties her to a post where hay hangs from a tree. I know this is one of the stops they take their clients, so the nice setup doesn't surprise me.

When he returns, he leads me to the table and unloads the food.

"You were serious about this date." I'm almost shocked as I meet his eyes.

"Of course. You thought I'd make a joke out of it, didn't you?"

I study him. "It's not over yet."

"Oh, SumSum." He pulls out the folding metal chair for me to sit in, then helps scoot me forward. "Sometimes you're adorably stubborn."

I place my hand over my heart and try to ignore the nickname only he calls me. "Could say the same about you."

"Oh, I'm purposely stubborn. There's no denying that."

117

Beckett opens the bottle of wine, then pours our clear plastic cups full. He hands mine over, and I take a sip. It's sweet and delicious, my favorite Chardonnay. Makes me wonder if Kinsley gave him some pointers.

Beckett lights a few tea candles on the table, then places plates with a cover in front of me. I remove the top and see fried chicken, green beans, and macaroni. My mouth instantly waters.

"You made this?"

"Yeah. Mama's recipe."

I smile. "Amazing."

Once he hands me plasticware and Beckett sits, we eat. The chicken is perfectly cooked, the macaroni is deliciously cheesy, and the green beans taste like they were cooked with bacon, just like Mrs. Valentine makes them. I'm shocked Beckett *can* cook this well.

"Why are you being so nice to me?" The question falls out when we finish eating. "Honestly, I thought you'd lead me here, and I dunno, attack me with water balloons, have a good laugh, then let me walk home in the dark soakin' wet."

His brow furrows. "Only an asshole would do that."

"Exactly my point."

"I understand you've got a bunch of preconceived notions about me, but I can guarantee you this, I respect women."

I laugh. "You haven't always respected me, Beckett. You've been pretty damn cruel."

His expression softens. "I'm sorry about that."

My mouth falls open, and I pinch myself. "Did you just apologize?"

He shrugs. "Yeah. I'm not tryin' to be a dickhead toward ya. Sometimes you get under my skin and try to piss me off, and it works."

A grin touches my lips. "You're right. I'm sorry, too. It's just easier to hate you."

"I can agree with that." Beckett places our empty plates

into the picnic basket. Then he removes another container and hands me another fork. "Dessert?"

He removes the lid, and I see two slices of quadruple-layered chocolate cake. My mouth falls open.

"Did Kinsley tell you to do this?"

He shakes his head. "No."

"How'd you know?" I dig my fork into the moist cake.

"Because I know you, Summer. Whether either of us wants to admit that or not. I know everything about you, and I'm sure you know a lot about me, too. We basically grew up together. I know you love autumn and not summer. If you had to choose between Kit Kat and Reese's, the peanut butter cups would win every single time. I know when you're lying or when you're mad. If you had to choose between the beach or a mountain trip, the mountains would win every time. And I know that you cried when you watched *The Lion King* for the first time."

I swallow hard, but I'm at a loss for words. It's true. I know everything about him, too. Things I probably shouldn't know, if I'm being honest.

"I didn't cry!"

He gives me a pointed look.

"Okay, maybe I did, but it was sad. I couldn't help it."

Beckett smiles. "How's the cake?"

"It's amazing. You made it, didn't you?"

"Yeah. I was busy this afternoon."

I take another bite. "Thank you."

"You're welcome."

Once we finish eating, Beckett cleans up, then grabs the bottle of wine and leads me over to the blanket by the firepit. He lights it, and the wood instantly catches and crackles. Beckett takes a seat next to me, and we sit cross-legged, watching the flames lick up toward the sky. The sun has fully set, but it's not completely dark yet.

The warmth of the fire feels great, and I find myself smiling.

"I owe you another apology." Beckett breaks the silence, his voice a hoarse whisper.

"For what?" I turn and meet his eyes.

"For beating the fuck out of Daniel."

I search his face, and we're sitting too close. The light from the fire splashes over us. "You don't have to apologize for that."

"I do. It wasn't my place to—"

"I owe you a thank-you, Beck. Fifteen-year-old me was embarrassed and pissed because it was the talk at school for months. Beckett Valentine beat the shit outta someone after prom because of me. Twenty-nine-year-old me understands that Daniel wanted to take advantage of me. I wasn't ready to have sex with him that night. I didn't even want to go to prom with him."

His brow furrows. "What?"

"I wanted to go with you."

His mouth falls open. "I...I...didn't know that."

"Once Hannah asked you, and you said yes, I knew it was over. A stupid childhood crush. I just wanted you to notice me, and I thought if I went with someone your age, you wouldn't see me as your little sister's best friend anymore. The whole thing was a mistake. Because after that night, things permanently changed between us."

He stares at the fire, not saying a word, soaking in everything I'm saying. It grows eerily quiet for a few minutes, and I think I've said too much.

"I would've taken you, Summer. I wanted to go with you. I just..." His words trail off, and he doesn't finish.

"Do you think that if I weren't Kinsley's best friend, things would've been different between us?"

A smirk hits his perfect lips. "No. But it's a nice thought. We are who we are regardless of Kinsley. Things would've probably still been the same."

I laugh. "You're right."

He turns to me. "But the past is in the past, Summer. All we have is right now and the future. It's up to us to change that."

When I meet his blue eyes, butterflies swarm in my belly. He studies my face, tucking loose strands of hair behind my ear.

"Kiss me," I whisper. "Please. I just…I have to know."

He scoots closer to me. "You're sure about this?"

"Yes," I say, my eyes fluttering closed.

14

BECKETT

$\mathcal{W}$hen Summer closes her eyes, I don't wait a moment to run my fingers through her hair and slide my lips across hers. At first, the kisses are small and slow, and she opens her mouth, giving me more access and permission. Her tongue dips into my mouth, massaging mine, and she moans.

I'm lost in the taste of the sweetness on her lips, and it takes every bit of strength I have to pull away. I don't want to, though. Emotions build and pour through me, and before I can create distance, she sucks on my bottom lip.

This is what wet dreams are made from, what I've fantasized about since I was a teenager, and after all these years, here we are, getting lost in each other.

Her eyes flutter open, her lips a swollen mess. I felt something while kissing her, something I'd never felt before— want and need, and an intense desire to have more.

They say some people get addicted after one hit...I understand that now more than ever. With just one kiss, Summer unlocked something deep inside me that's been dormant for an eternity. It was just a kiss, but a kiss has never overpowered me like that before.

She places her fingers over her lips and meets my eyes. There's no way she didn't feel that.

The silence between us grows loud, and I can't find the proper words.

"That was…" She doesn't finish her sentence.

Neither of us is thinking straight, our heads are a woozy mess, and my cock is hard as hell.

I grab the bottle of wine, pop the cork, and place it to my lips before passing it to Summer. She chugs, taking four big gulps before handing it back to me.

We crossed a line, one we've skirted for over a decade, and I have no regrets.

I got the answer to my question, and now I know it's more than just a stupid childhood crush.

I felt something wild and intense.

Summer Jones is intoxicating in all the right ways.

I stand, adding more wood to the fire. Now that the sun has set, the temperature is dropping. Once the flames lick up toward the sky again, I sit beside her.

Summer removes her boots and socks, allowing the fire to warm her toes, then lies flat on her back and stares up at the sky. I do the same and join her. It's so clear tonight, and the stars are bright.

"That right there, the C—that's the Corona Borealis constellation. You can only see it in the summer months. A lot of different myths and legends go with it. The Greeks saw it as a crown. But my favorite is what the Shawnee tribe believed." I stare up at it. "Each star represents a dancing maiden. It's an incomplete circle because one fell in love with a mortal warrior, and she left the sky to live with him on earth."

"A C of stars in a sea of stars." She looks up at it, then turns to face me. "I have a confession."

I look into her eyes, having no idea what she's going to say, and my heart hammers hard in my chest.

Summer breathes in deeply through her nose and then exhales. "I don't hate you."

I laugh, reaching over and running my fingers through her brown hair. "I don't hate you, either. However, you're a gigantic pain in my ass."

"Oh, same. Don't get it twisted." She smiles, leaning forward to take control, and slides her perfect lips against mine again.

"Don't start somethin' you can't finish," I growl against her mouth, fisting her hair before she slides her tongue against mine again. I sit up, laying her back down, kissing her like this might be the first and last opportunity of my life to do so.

Then I trail kisses from her cheek to her ear and trace the shell with my mouth. She sighs when I place my hand under her shirt against the warmth of her bare stomach.

"I've always wanted you, Summer." I admit my truths. "But you've got to meet me halfway."

"I can't be another notch on your headboard, Beck."

Hearing my nickname on her lips nearly makes me lose it. I know she's serious when she shows me the girl she often hides from the world. The Summer I fell for all those years ago.

"That would never happen." She sits up, resting herself on her elbows. "Is it selfish of me to want you?"

"Hell no. Is it selfish of me to want to make you feel good?"

She brings her hand forward and wraps it around my neck, crashing our lips together. "I think that's the first time a man has ever said that to me."

"If you were mine…"

With one hand, I undo the top button of her jeans and slide the zipper down. She lies back, her breathing increasing, causing her breasts to rise and fall.

"I'd please you every night." I slide my fingers inside her panties, and she's so fucking wet I can't stand it. She lets out a small pant as I kiss her, rubbing light circles against her needy little bud.

"Beck. That feels so good." Her voice is ragged and desperate.

I've barely touched her, and she's nearly unraveling. My cock is ready to snap in two as it fills my jeans. I adjust myself and return inside her panties, then dip a finger inside her pussy, which immediately clenches around me. I pull my fingers out and place them in my mouth. "Fuck, you taste so damn good."

She looks at me with hooded eyes. "I do?"

"Yes. Sweet. And you're so goddamn wet for me."

Summer licks her lips. "I've waited for this for a long time."

I kiss her softly. "I'm not fuckin' you tonight, SumSum."

She looks...*disappointed.*

"Not because I don't want to." I glance down at my hard-as-steel cock, and so does she. "Tonight wasn't about that."

"I know," she mutters.

"But I'd like to make you feel good."

"Okay." She smiles, kissing me again.

"But not with my fingers."

Her eyes widen.

"I need to *taste* more of you, sweetheart."

She swallows hard, standing, and wiggles her jeans down to her ankles. I'm basically on my knees for her as I remove them from her body. I'm face-to-face with her pink lace panties. My palms trail up her thighs, and I look into her eyes. She's smirking as I reach around and grab her ass. Summer steadies herself using my shoulders as I grab the single string holding them to her body and rip them off.

She yelps. "Hey!"

"Keepsake, because I know you wore them for me."

I see her blush, and she doesn't deny it.

"Pink is my favorite color." I lift them to my nose and smell them before shoving them into my pocket. As she stands above me, I admire her pretty little pussy, which is completely shaven.

"You sure we're alone out here?" she asks nervously, looking around. The light from the fire gives me the perfect view of her beautiful body.

I nod. "As far as I know. Just me, you, Pebbles, and the stars."

She meets my eyes. "I've just…never fooled around outside."

"First time for everything, sweetheart. Relax. You're tense."

A laugh escapes her. "I'm nervous."

"Why?" I slide my hands up her shirt, and she unbuttons it for me, allowing it to fall on the blanket. Then she reaches behind her and undoes her bra.

I'm at a loss for words as I look up and study her—she's pure perfection. Summer Jones is a Southern goddess, and I'm on my knees, ready to worship every inch of her. Even if I'm not worthy.

Goose bumps cover her skin as my calloused hands lift her thigh and place it over my shoulder. Slowly, I twirl my tongue against her clit and then lick down to her opening before fully devouring her.

"Fuck," she hisses as I reach up and twist her nipple.

Just the smell of her arousal, the soft pants of her breathing, and the way she rides my face have me so damn addicted, I'm not sure one date will be enough.

"Beck." She whispers my name as I reach around, steadying her ass. She threads her fingers through my hair, her head falling back on her neck.

"You wanna lie down, sweetheart?"

"Please." Her legs tremble. I pull away, leaving her dripping wet.

Carefully, she lies back on the blanket, and I move up to her mouth, slowly kissing her, allowing her to taste her arousal. "I think you've become my new favorite flavor."

She lifts a brow as I slide my lips down her body and position myself between her legs. I dip one digit inside her tight walls, her pussy clenching for me.

"Fuck." I grunt, adding another digit. "You're so gorgeous."

She sighs, her body arching as I wage war against her cunt.

"So…close." Her words are barely audible as her hips buck against my face.

I pull away, licking my lips. "You'll come when I let you."

She pushes herself up on her elbows and glares at me. The underlying threat in her gaze makes my cock twitch as she slides her hand down to her clit and begins working herself.

"Got to admit, that's sexy as fuck, but this pussy is mine tonight." I push her hand away and smack her cunt. "You'll come when I say."

"Or maybe I won't come at all." She shrugs. "Maybe you don't have what it takes."

"Oh, sweetheart." I slide two digits inside her and then place them in my mouth. "You're so fuckin' close I can taste it."

Once my mouth is back between her legs, she returns to her back, opening her thighs wide for me. With each flick of my tongue, she writhes under me, her pants growing more frustrated each time I bring her to the edge and leave her hanging.

When I gently suck her sensitive bud, then plunge my fingers inside her tight walls, she moans.

"Let me come." She's a panting, dripping-wet diva.

I work her as slow as molasses, taking my own sweet time as the orgasm builds. Her back arches, and her pants grow more guttural as she tweaks her nipples.

She screams, "Yes, yes, yes!"

When she finally spills over the edge, she says my name, and the sound of her voice echoes throughout the trees. Her pussy throbs around my fingers as she fists my hair, riding my scruffy face and taking what she needs.

I give her control, then flick my tongue against her clit. It's obvious how sensitive it is, but she doesn't force me to stop. And then, minutes later, she's coming again.

"Good girl," I whisper. "Two in a row."

She laughs.

I click my tongue. "Shall we go for three?"

"Yes." She squeezes her thighs together before presenting herself to me again. "Beck. I wish you'd fuck me."

I push three digits inside, then continue licking and flicking that clit. "Mmm," I hum against her. "Don't tempt me with a good time, sweetheart."

She huffs. "Never woulda thought you'd deny me."

I add more pressure, loving how she writhes under my tongue. "It's not denial, Summer. You're just not the kinda girl I'd fuck and forget about."

She pops back up onto her elbows, lookin' at me. "You gettin' all sensitive on me, now?"

I chuckle. "Just keeping it real. Now come on my face. Third time's a charm."

She moans as I continue to tease her, and when she completely unravels again, I lick up every last drop. Her head falls to the side, and she closes her thighs. I lie beside her, brushing hair from her face, then press a soft kiss on her lips.

"You're so fuckin' sexy."

"Could say the same about you." Her eyes flutter closed. "No one has ever—and I mean, *ever*—given me three in a row."

"Not even you?"

She blushes. "Maybe."

"I'd love to watch you touch yourself."

She smiles. "I bet you would. But I have another confession to make. I don't like it soft and gentle. I enjoy being fucked, my ass smacked, and my hair pulled. I'm not a fragile little doll, Beck." Her hand slides down to my cock, which might snap into two at this point.

I gently grab her wrist.

"Tonight was about you, Summer. I can't."

"Rejection." Her whisper floats in the early summer breeze.

"It's not." I shake my head, not ready to fully admit how

I've always felt about her. The lines are already too blurred. But I don't want her to do anything she'll regret. Fooling around is different. I know once I've had her, I won't ever let her go, and I'm not sure she's ready for that. Even now, I struggle with what tomorrow will bring for us.

"Thank you." She slides her jeans over her bare ass, puts on her bra and shirt, then sits beside me. I open my arm, allowing her to lean into me, taking in my warmth.

"Oh, look." She points up, and I catch the tail end of a meteor glittering across the sky.

"Make a wish," I whisper, making my own.

As the fire dies down, she lets out a yawn. I check the time. It's late, and we're both early risers. Our night together is ending, and while I don't want it to be over, it is.

"We should probably get goin'." I clean up around the site and pour water from the pond onto the fire, then she unties Pebbles. I climb on, scooting behind the saddle, then she joins me. I wrap my arms around her waist, allowing her to lead us back to the house.

During the ride, I place soft kisses on her neck, and she giggles, leaning into me. I want to ask her where we go from here and what tomorrow will bring, but I don't want to pressure her. I suppose I'll be patient. It's in her hands now.

We make our way to her cabin, where she's left the porch light on. She unsaddles, and I slide off and walk her to her door.

"I hope you had a good night." I lean in and trace my lips across hers.

She pours herself into me, and I nearly lose control right there against her front door. Somehow, I stop.

"You too. Now, about that bid."

I laugh. "Oh yeah."

I lean in, whispering the number in her ear before sucking on the bottom of her earlobe. When I pull away and meet her eyes, she beams. "Have a good night, Beck."

"You too."

She opens her mouth to say something, then quickly closes it. Then she turns and walks inside. I place my hand on my heart, which feels as if it's ready to explode from my chest, and force myself to walk away.

The ride home is agonizing.

I take Pebbles to the barn, unsaddle her, give her some treats, then put her in the stable. She's had a long night, but she's used to doing midnight excursions during our cowboy day celebrations.

As soon as I get home, I shower and roughly stroke my cock, needing to get her out of my system. Summer Jones whispered my name tonight, begging me to let her come. That's a moment I will never forget for the rest of my life, even if it's the only one I'll ever share with her like that.

15

SUMMER

*T*he following morning, I stretch my legs, waking before my alarm sounds. A smile touches my lips, and I halfway wonder if last night happened or if it was a figment of my fantasies.

I see my jeans, boots, and shirt I wore lying on the floor in a pile. All of it was...*real.* And while I enjoyed the fuck out of Beckett devouring me and making me come three times in a row, I'm not sure if we should ever cross that line again.

When my alarm goes off, I crawl out of bed and feed the animals. I make quick work of it, which I'm happy about because I have the rest of the day to myself. Now that I know Beckett's offer, I need to get in touch with Natalie and raise my bid to at least $100,000 higher than his, and I'll add just a little extra for good measure.

Once I'm home, I run a hot bubble bath. I strip out of my clothes and slide inside the water, the heat feeling amazing between my legs. Though Beckett's fingers were the only thing inside me, I'm sore. I can only imagine what kind of damage his cock would've done.

Before I get too lost in my thoughts, my cell phone buzzes

on the side of the tub. I flick water off my hands, then pick it up.

> Are you alive? Hello?

I chuckle. Shit, I forgot to text her last night and this morning. I've been too busy floating on cloud nine.

> Yes, your brother didn't murder me and throw my body into the pond.

> Thank God. So? How was the sex?

My cheeks heat, and I wonder if she knows or if she's making jokes. I mean, could she know? Should I tell her? The last thing I want to do is hide anything from her, but I'm not sure if I'm ready to admit what we did. So I keep it general. Not necessarily a lie, but not the complete truth either.

> Your brother didn't fuck me.

> But you would've let him, right?

> Hush up.

> 🙄 You would've. You have to tell me all about it, considering he was so secretive. Wanna meet me at the bakery? I could go for one of Sadie's stuffed kolaches with jalapeños.

I check the time. It's barely past ten.

> Sure. But I need to be at the coffee shop after 12. I have a new bid to submit.

> He told you?

> Yep! I earned it fair and square.

Yeah, you did. Okay, I'll meet you there in thirty. That good?

Perfect.

I finish bathing, wash my hair, then get out of the tub. I throw on a comfy old blue jean skirt and a T-shirt that says Bless Your Heart. I head to town, and Kinsley arrives at the same time.

"I'm so hungry right now, I could eat a horse." She opens the door, and the cowbell hits, alerting everyone of our arrival.

Some heads turn, but almost everyone is lost in their own conversations. When we walk in, Sadie, the owner, greets us from behind the counter. We patiently wait in the small line of people, looking at everything she made fresh this morning behind the glass case. I didn't realize I was so starving until now.

Her best friend, Hazel, works the cash register, and when we walk up, Sadie's bright red lips turn up into a wide smile showing her perfect teeth.

"How're you ladies doin'?" Her golden eyes soften when she speaks to us.

"Doin' fine. Geez, Sadie. I love that color on you." The royal purple looks gorgeous against her black skin. But then again, Sadie makes any color look good. She's beautiful, with mid-length braids and one of the most contagious laughs I've ever heard. The woman is pure sunshine.

She's a few years older than us and graduated from high school when we were still in junior high. Her family has done a lot for the community. Her mama is the whole reason the food bank even exists in the county.

"Don't flatter me this early in the day." Sadie playfully waves us off. "Might have to spoil you with a chocolate-covered donut."

"She won't complain about that. Your donuts are next level and addictin'," I admit.

"Thank you. So whatcha havin' today?"

"I want two jalapeño kolaches, a pig in a blanket, and I will take one of those chocolate éclairs. A coffee, too. The big fat one."

Sadie chuckles as she writes the order down on a small notepad.

"I'll do a sausage and egg croissant, and I'll take a big-ass coffee, too."

"And you're both gettin' a donut." She gives us a wink.

"You know I can't resist." The chocolate is caked on top, and I think I might eat it first.

Sadie puts our items onto a silver platter and meets us at the end of the counter. She hands our order to Hazel, who rings us up as Sadie pours our coffee.

"Thank you!" Kinsley and I say in unison, and she grins. "Don't be strangers, ya hear?"

We nod, pay, then make our way to one of the small tables in the corner so we can have privacy in the cozy space. Just after we sit, we add cream and sugar to our cups and sip. We both release a sigh at the same time.

Ethel, one of the town's gossip leaders, asks Sadie when she's getting married, and I groan.

I lean over and meet Kinsley's eyes. "I seriously hate that question."

"Same. Also, we all know Sadie doesn't need a man. A man needs *her*."

I laugh hard. "You're right. She's independent and successful. I want to be just like her when I grow up."

"Oh, you will be. Especially when you put your new bid in and win the Horseshoe Creek Ranch. Speaking of my brother..."

She lingers, and of course, my cheeks turn bright red, giving me away.

Her mouth falls open. "You better tell me *everything*."

I try to speak, but no words come out. Kinsley tears into her kolache with wide eyes, impatiently waiting for me to spill the beans.

"Summer!" she stresses around a mouthful.

"I'm fixin' to tell you, just gimme a minute. Shit." I try to gather my words, knowing my face will give me away if I leave any details out. She's too observant. Sometimes it's a blessing, but it's a curse when it comes to things like this.

She swallows and impatiently taps her fingers on the table.

I look around, not wanting to be overheard, and speak in a hushed tone. "He picked me up at the house on a horse."

"Seriously?" I'm unsure why she's surprised. Beckett loves to ride. It's always been his thing and always will be.

"What's wrong with that?"

She shrugs. "It's boring."

"It wasn't, though. Dare I say, I had a good time."

Her mouth falls open with a gasp. "No."

I tuck my bottom lip into my mouth.

"Did you bang?"

I can't even get a word out.

"Oh my God, you did!"

"Not technically." I'm feeling self-conscious with too many wandering eyes.

"Okay, so he picked you up on horseback, then what?"

I tell her how we took the trail to the pond, and he had prepared dinner for us. I chat about the fire and the blanket, and even the stars.

"And then?"

I lift a brow. "Then I gave him dessert."

Her eyes are wide.

"I don't know what came over me. I guess it was the Valentine charm. We didn't have sex. He just went down…" I dart my eyes down between my legs and then back to her. "And I let him."

135

Her mouth falls open. "Okay, like I don't want to know any details, but…how was it?"

"Incredible."

"I knew it. I fuckin' knew it!" Her loud voice bounces off the walls. When Ethel turns and looks at her for cussing, Kinsley goes back to a quieter speaking voice.

"So what does this mean? Are you two…together? Dating? Wedding bells in the future?"

"Geez, Kinsley. No. It means we fooled around. I had a few O's, and that's it."

"Wait. A *few*?"

I shrug. "Three. He's good at what he does. I mean…*really* good."

"And I think I just threw up in my mouth." She's smiling, though. "So are you two pretending you still hate each other or what? Must give you both a boner, considering you're so dead set on the world knowing you're enemies. But I know the truth. Always have. And I seriously cannot wait to deliver a big shiny *I TOLD YOU SO* to his face."

"Please don't. I'm pretending it didn't happen, and so should you. I'm convinced we just got caught up in the moment. The stars, the wine, all of it. Nothing was forced, and it all just happened naturally. It pains me to admit it, but it was one of the best dates I've had in my life."

"But what if you didn't just get caught up in the moment? What if he's the one for you? The man you've been lookin' for all this time?"

I laugh. "And what if cows fly? What if I win the lottery tomorrow? What if I get struck by lightning the next time it rains? What-ifs don't matter, Kinsley. "

"But what if, in this instance, they do?" She's wearing a cheeky grin.

I check the time on my phone. She's hounded me about Beckett for a good twenty-five minutes while we've finished eating.

"You want half of this éclair?"

I happily take the offer because it's so damn good.

Before we leave, we wave goodbye to Sadie, then make our way down to the coffee shop.

I stop by my Jeep to grab the envelope with the new bid inside, and I have to admit, I'm feeling pretty confident about this.

"Is that the winner?" Kinsley glances at the envelope.

A huge smile fills my face. "I hope so."

We walk past the small park in the middle of the town square. It's where all of the holiday celebrations are held. The grass is green and lush, and I'm tempted to lie in it when the sun shines like this. I check the time, realizing we're still a little early, so the two of us find a bench and finish drinking our coffees.

"Do you think Natalie will be there today?"

Kinsley gives me a pointed look. "She's there every day. It's the only way she can connect to the real world."

"That's a blessing, honestly. Makes it so easy to just run into her. But then again, makes me realize when the B&B is up and runnin', I'll need to find a way for guests to connect to the internet."

Kinsley laughs. "Did you notice what you said?"

I shake my head.

"You said *when* the B&B is running. Not if. Speaking it into existence!" She holds up her palm to give me a high five, and I slap my hand against hers.

"I didn't even realize." I look down at the envelope in my hands. "I feel great about this. It just seems like it's all coming together now that I know how much I need to offer. It's mine."

"Yes, girl! That's the spirit." She downs the rest of her coffee. "I think I'mma need a refill. Luckily, we're about to walk into a place that sells exactly what I'm lookin' for."

I finish mine too. "I think I'm caffeinated out. With all the excitement running through me, I feel as if I'm buzzing."

"Or maybe that's the aftereffects of my brother's mouth?"

I bump my shoulder against hers. "Honey, hush."

"It's true. They say orgasms are a stress reliever. Wouldn't be surprised if you feel like a million bucks after...how many did you say?"

"Three."

She shakes her head. "Damn. He's like a genie in a bottle granting three orgasms like they're wishes."

I smile. "Yeah, it was enough to last me a little while at least."

"What? You've got to see him again."

"No. If it happens, it happens. I'm not putting in any effort. But anyway, enough about me. What about the internet dude?"

She shrugs. "I asked him to send me a dick pic last night, and it was too small."

I snort. "Seriously?"

Kinsley stretches out her pinky. "This is bigger."

I gasp.

"But...I did see Luca last night."

"Whoa. The bartender? He said he wants to go back to New York."

"So what? I'm not looking for a husband. I'm searching for fun."

"Yeah, yeah, whatever you say. This is exactly how people fall in love and get their hearts broken."

"We talked until four in the mornin'. He's made it very clear that he's only stayin' through the summer. I'm looking forward to a fling. A younger man who has stamina in and outside of the bedroom."

"How old is he?"

"Twenty-one. Old enough." She winks.

I shake my head. "Come September, I don't want to hear you cryin' over this."

"You'd listen, though."

"I would, but I just don't want you to get hurt."

"I'm not going to fall in love. Trust me. After Hayden, that part of my heart is dead."

The light breeze brushes against my cheeks, and I nearly shiver. "Speaking of him…"

"No. I don't want to speak of him. Fuck him."

I pat her thigh and give her a small smile. "I know. And you're right. Fuck him."

Kinsley was in love with that man, and we all believed they'd get married and spend their lives together. But he moved away, dumped her, got engaged to another woman, and he's been dead to Kinsley ever since. Some people never get over heartbreak like that, and I'm not sure she ever will.

Ever since Hayden, she hasn't been able to keep a relationship. The ghost of him and what they had still haunts her, even if she doesn't talk about it. However, there are those random times when she gets too drunk for her own good, and it all spills out. I listen because that's what friends do, but I know she's still hurt. Hell, I'd be, too, especially after everything they went through together.

"Well, I hope you have an amazing summer full of flirting and fucking."

"Thanks, friend. You too."

I snort. "No, don't wish that upon me."

"Too late for all that. And this time, I didn't start it and didn't even have to play matchmaker. You chose it when you let my brother's face between your legs."

This has me snickering. "Shut up. I have no regrets."

"I wouldn't either. If that happened to me, I'd let Jesus take the wheel 'cause I'd be dyin' from pleasure."

I burst into a full-blown belly laugh, but she's not wrong. It was mind-altering, and I'm not sure I've fully recovered from Beckett's tongue and mouth, but I keep that inside.

Kinsley looks over her shoulder. "Oh, look. There's Natalie right now." She points at the ranch truck she drives around. "We'll give her five minutes to settle, then walk over."

"Sounds good." I let out a long, slow breath. "I just got super nervous."

"Oh gosh, don't be. You've got this."

"Yeah, yeah."

We make small talk, allowing the clock to tick. When Kinsley stands and stretches, I know it's go time. We walk into the coffee shop, and the smell of freshly roasted coffee fills the room. Immediately, Kinsley waves at Natalie, then orders a latte. Once Kinsley has her second big-ass coffee for the day, she leads the way over.

"What a coincidence. We were just chatting about you." Kinsley takes a sip.

"Oh?" Natalie looks back and forth between us.

"Yeah." I pull the envelope from my back pocket. "I wanted to submit another bid."

Natalie holds out her hand with a grin. "Fantastic."

She opens the envelope in front of us, just like she did the last time, and instead of her smile growing, it fades.

Kinsley clears her throat. "Oh no. What's wrong?"

"Nothing." Her voice slightly lowers. "Beckett changed his bid this morning as well. Unfortunately, this won't beat his."

Kinsley's brow furrows, and a wave of anger surges through me so fast that I nearly scream out with frustration.

"What did you say?" I ask, making sure I didn't misunderstand her.

"This bid won't beat Beckett's. I'm sorry, Summer. I just met up with him about an hour ago."

"That bastard! I'm going to kill him." I clench my jaw tight.

Natalie gives me a look, and it grows awkward.

I force a smile. "Thank you so much. I appreciate it. I know you don't have to tell me those things."

She blinks up at me. "I'm so sorry."

I thank her again and leave the coffee shop. Kinsley stays inside, chatting with her for a little longer as I try to breathe in

140

the fresh air while I pace outside. I should've known he wouldn't have made this easy. I should've fucking known.

My heart rate increases, and my entire body feels hot.

I'm spiraling and find a bench at the end of the sidewalk, outside the closed beauty shop, and sit. Five minutes later, Kinsley joins me.

"I can't believe this. Now what are we going to do?"

"He tricked me! I'm going to kick his ass!"

Kinsley meets my eyes. "Honestly, he deserves it after that. It's messed up."

"I'm so mad, Kins."

"I can tell. You're shakin'." She reaches over and grabs my hand. "What do you want me to do? Anything. Just ask."

"I want him hog-tied and on my porch waiting for me to tar and feather him."

She snickers. "He'd never let us capture him. Not even if I could get Harrison, Colt, and Emmett on board."

"Then I guess I'll have to do it myself." I stand and make my way down the sidewalk.

"Wait." She runs after me. "If you need any help, let me know."

"Just find out where he is and I'll take care of the rest."

Kinsley nods. "That's a deal."

16

BECKETT

"*S*ure thing, Mrs. Flores," I say. "I'll put you on the schedule for next week, and we can start lessons on balancing while trotting."

"Sounds great, thank ya."

I walk her to her Cadillac, which is parked right up front. She's seventy, moved to the country after her husband died, and decided she wanted to take private riding lessons. It's been a pleasure teaching her, though sometimes she talks in riddles like Yoda or something.

As soon as she backs out of the driveway, I wave goodbye.

The day has been long and hard, and the sun is setting just over the horizon.

I head back into the stables to unsaddle Tinker Bell. Just as I remove the bridle, then slide the saddle and pad off the horse, I catch a glance of headlights against the far wall. A moment later, I hear someone parking beside the barn, followed by a door slamming.

Whoever it is, they're storming across the gravel like they're on a rampage. Probably Harrison getting ready to start the afternoon feedings since it's his turn, and he probably has plans. What else is new, though?

To be twentysomething again without a care in the damn world.

"You *bastard*!"

As soon as I hear Summer's shrieking voice, I chuckle.

"So nice to see you, too." I turn, meeting her cold gaze.

Her fists are in tight balls, and she looks like she might punch my lights out.

I grab the brush and continue with Tinker Bell. I don't care if she's seething. I have a job to finish.

"What the hell is wrong with you?" There's a tremble in her voice because her anger is getting the best of her.

"Ain't nothin' wrong with me. How 'bout you? Somethin' eatin' away atcha?"

She lets out a deep growl, and I find it adorably cute.

"Stop playin' stupid. You tricked me!"

"Nah. We never made a deal that I couldn't change my bid after I gave you my first number. Guess you're not smarter than the average bear."

I lead Tinker Bell to the pasture, and she walks away without a care in the world.

"You're an asshole!" Summer yells. I make my way toward her. She crosses her arms over her chest with her feet firmly planted, standing her ground.

"Did you think it'd be that easy?" I laugh, and I know I'm skirting the line. Honestly can't remember the last time I saw her this angry.

Her breath hitches as her eyes trail up and down my body. For a moment, I forget she's raging pissed and wonder if she's thinking about last night.

I haven't been able to get her off my mind all day.

She uncrosses her arms and pushes her finger hard into my chest. "You're an arrogant bastard."

"And? Wouldn't be surprised if your panties are dripping wet right now. You seem to like that shit."

"Fuck you, Beckett. This isn't a game to me."

"Oh, I'm not playin' games, SumSum. I'm clearly winning that property whether you and your pretty little pussy like that or not."

"I hate you. I hate you so goddamn much."

"That's not what you said when I was buried between your legs last night. If I recall, you quite enjoyed yourself. *Three times*." I walk away from her, grab the brush, and take it to the tack room.

She swiftly follows me. "Why're ya doin' this?"

I set the brush onto the counter, then wash my hands in the sink. She impatiently waits for me to finish, then I turn to her. I take several steps forward, and she backs up until her body presses up against the wall. "Doin' what, Summer?"

"Drivin' me fucking crazy."

I stare into her eyes, unspoken words streaming between us. Her nostrils flare, and I know she's livid, but that doesn't stop me from caging her in with my arms.

Leaning down to whisper in her ear, I say, "I can't control the way you feel."

Slowly, I trace the shell of her ear with my lips. Her breathing increases, and she tightly fists my shirt.

"Asshole."

She may be seething, but I notice how quickly her body responds to me. As I stare into her eyes, waiting for her to continue her onslaught of cuss words, she glances down at my cock. Hard as concrete.

She puckers her lips. "Looks like you're getting a little too much enjoyment out of this."

I move closer, my face a breath away from hers. "And I'd bet the Horseshoe Creek Ranch that you're fuckin' drippin'."

Her lips crash against mine with a vengeance as she roughly threads her fingers through my hair and tugs hard.

"You're such a fuckin' asshole." Our kisses grow more heated. I'm holding her thigh up with one hand, steadying her with the other.

"And you're a very, *very* fuckin' bad girl."

She unbuckles my belt with a yank, unbuttons my jeans, then forcefully unzips me. My cock throbs for her, and when she grabs me through my boxers, her eyes go wide.

"You're pierced?"

I shrug. "I lost a bet."

She makes a face. "To who?"

"Your bestie." I lift the skirt she's wearing and dip my hands into her thin panties. When I slide my fingers between her folds, she releases a long sigh. "Drenched, just like I thought."

I tuck my fingertips into my mouth, tasting her sweetness, remembering exactly what I had last night.

"I hate that I want you. You piss me off!" Her tongue swipes against mine as she pushes my boxers down. "I hate it so much."

Her hair is thrown up in a ponytail, and I wrap it around my fist, forcing her to look into my eyes. "Your body says otherwise."

Summer's stroking up and down my shaft, and I know if she doesn't stop, we'll never be able to go back to how things were. Hell, we might already be past the point of no return.

I drop down to my knees, forcing her little blue jean skirt up around her waist and pushing down her panties. She widens her legs just enough to give me space to lick that clit.

"Greedy as fuck." I slide my tongue into her pussy, slurping up every drop of her arousal. She's just showered; the sugary smell of her berry-scented bodywash encapsulates me as I devour her like she's my last meal. Summer rocks her hips as she roughly tugs my hair, riding my face. The other hand pinches her pebbled nipple.

"Show me."

She lifts her shirt on my demand. She didn't even bother putting on a bra.

"If I didn't know better, I'd say you planned this shit."

"Fuck," she screams, "you!"

I smirk, sliding two digits inside her tight pussy. "Don't forget, I fuckin' love that smart mouth."

"Beck." She trembles when I push a third finger inside. She's already so fucking close to coming, and I leave her suspended in the air, teetering on the edge.

"Don't you dare come," I growl against her inner thigh.

"Let me."

"Hell no." I slow my pace.

A deep moan releases from her as I wage war against her pussy, licking and sucking her clit, tickling that G-spot. When she comes, I hope she crumples. Her entire body shakes, her perfect tits trembling as she impatiently waits on edge.

I give her one long lick, and she explodes. I remove my fingers and tongue-fuck her. "Damn, baby."

Her body slides down the wall, and she opens her legs for me, letting me see that wet cunt clench. Summer looks up at me with hooded eyes, and then they're filled with alarm.

"Did you hear that?"

We both stop moving, and I swear we stop breathing, too, and then I hear Harrison whistling. "Beckett!"

"Shit." We say it at the same time. I look around the room, then my eyes meet Summer's.

I shake my head, pulling up my jeans and repositioning myself. "I swear to fuck, he has the worst timing on the planet. The worst."

"I need to hide!" She panics as his voice comes closer. "Go, go…entertain him or something. He can't come in here."

That's when I smirk. "In here!"

Summer bolts up and ducks behind a few saddle horses. She lifts her middle fingers in the air and then brings them down when the door swings open.

I chuckle as she calls me a bastard.

Harrison enters and looks around. "Why does it smell like sex in here?"

This causes me to burst into laughter. "Probably your upper lip."

He shrugs. "Could be. Anyway. You gonna tell me about your date last night with Summer?"

The thought of her hiding in this very room has me grinning.

Harrison must notice my expression. "Oh, it was good, then?"

"Eh, it was fine."

"Did she put out?"

I bet she's ready to explode. "Nah."

"Yeah, didn't think she would. She's too uptight. Probably sewn shut down there."

I slam him hard on the back. "Better than being split wide open, though."

"True. So did you tell her how much you're in love with her and how you used to jac—"

"Harrison. Shut the fuck up. What do you think?"

"No, 'cause you're too much of a dipshit. One day she's going to marry someone, and you're gonna be a big ole pussy about it, cryin' that your girl got away. And I don't want to hear it when it happens. You've had plenty of opportunities to get in her panties. Plenty."

"Oh, you're absolutely right." I laugh, knowing Summer is squirming.

He shakes his head at me. "You're being weird as fuck. Get laid or something. Anyway, I gotta feed the horses. I'm meeting up with someone later at the bar."

"It's a Sunday."

"And?" He gives me a puzzled look.

"Don't you ever give your dick a day of rest?"

He chuckles. "Good one. The answer is no."

I suck in a breath. "Didn't think so. Anyway, probably gonna head out in a bit. See ya bright and early tomorrow?"

"Yeah." His phone rings, and he answers it on speaker. Of course, it's the woman he's meeting later. Harrison moves to the entryway, and moments later, Summer slowly stands, giving me her death glare.

"What the fuck was that?"

I shrug and rush over to her, then plant my lips on hers. "Come home with me."

She studies my face, searching my eyes, waiting for me to laugh or make a joke. "Wait. You're serious?"

My fingers find their way up her skirt and between her legs. "If we don't get each other out of our systems, we're going to keep fuckin' doin' this."

Her brow pops. "Doin' what?"

I slide two fingers inside her, and she grabs my arms, steadying herself. Her head rolls back on her shoulders, and I know if I added just enough pressure to her clit, she'd lose herself again right here on my hand.

"I'll give you ten more seconds, and then the opportunity is gonna pass you by forever," I state, counting slowly in her ear, rubbing my thumb faster against her clit.

"One."

She pants, sinking onto my fingers, but I keep up my pace, seeing her heartbeat tick faster in her chest.

"Two." I kiss up the side of her neck. She grows more breathless, more desperate.

"Beckett."

"Three." I trace the shell of her ear with my mouth, and as the orgasm continues to build, I keep counting.

When I hit the number "nine," she's dripping wet, and I pull away. "That's a shame."

I turn and head toward the door.

"Wait." She pushes down her skirt. Her lips are a swollen mess, and her hair is in a lopsided ponytail. "I want you."

I look at her incredulously. "Pretty sure you wanted to destroy me about thirty minutes ago."

She nods, and I lean in and grab her bottom lip between my teeth and suck.

"Mmm. I still do. But I need this. I just need you to know it means nothin'. Got it?"

I shrug. "Whatever you say. There are no strings attached, SumSum. Only rope. Tied around your wrists and ankles, attaching you to my bedpost."

Her brow lifts; she's intrigued. "Is that a promise?"

"It can be." I grab her ass. "Where'd you park?"

"On the side, over here by the fence."

"Okay, you're parked in a blind spot, then. I'll go out first and let you know if my brother is around. Then meet me out the side door, where my truck is."

"This is ridiculous. Why are we sneakin' around?"

I meet her gaze. "You want Harrison to know you're going home with me? If so, then feel free to lead the fuckin' way."

"You're right. His mouth is too big. The plan is on."

"Alright." I don't know why a bolt of adrenaline rushes through me. It could be because I'm going to worship Summer all night or the fact that Harrison could catch us. Either way, I don't hesitate when I walk out, and I try to keep my cool.

I can hear him in the feed room on the phone, and I wave for Summer to join me. I hold out my hand, and that's when I hear Harrison call my name. We run to the side door and hop into my truck. I start the engine, back out, and peel off.

Summer smiles and leans her head against the seat, then turns to look at me. "How many women have you brought back to your place in the past year?"

I laugh. "Countin' you?"

"One."

"No way. I don't believe you."

I shrug. "You don't have to. I ain't got nothin' to prove."

She looks shocked, though.

"Why is that so hard to believe?"

"Plenty of women try to get in your pants."

"Doesn't mean I let them. I'm done fucking for fun…you're the exception," I admit.

"Aw, I feel special. Thanks for giving me the opportunity." The sarcasm drips in her tone.

"Keep runnin' that smart mouth, and I'mma have to put something in it to shut you up."

"Big threats from a…" She glances down at my cock, which is nearly ready to rip my jeans open. "Big man."

"Not sure if you can handle this, sweetheart. Gonna take you on the ride of your life."

"What's that sayin'?" she asks. "Save a horse——"

"Reverse cowgirl," I interrupt. "It's always the answer."

We pull up to my house and get out of the truck. I leave my door unlocked since I live in the middle of nowhere, and we make our way inside.

Summer walks around, looking at the pictures of me and my brothers and sisters that are framed and set up on a table by the door. I throw my keys on top of it.

"Aw, I remember this." She looks at a picture of me, her, and Kinsley before things went south between us.

"Yeah?" I lean in, getting a better look. "Fourth of July when I was seventeen."

"Fourth of July. Fourteen. The night you *almost* kissed me."

My eyes soften as I meet her gaze. "So is that when the crush started for you?"

She reaches back and playfully smacks my arm. "That was the moment I knew you were a prick."

I take a step closer, wrapping my arms around her. "A prick who will spend all night on his knees making it up to you."

"Ya know, I kinda like the thought of that."

I push her against the door and place kisses across her neck until I meet her mouth. "As much as I'd like to fuck you right here, I need a shower. Wanna join me?"

"I already showered, but it's one of my *favorite* places to be."

I grab her hand and lead her to the bathroom. Carefully, I slide the shirt off her body, revealing her hard nipples and supple breasts. I suck each one, twisting my tongue around the hard peaks, then slide her little skirt off her body. She kicks off her shoes and stands naked before me.

"You're so fuckin' beautiful, Summer."

She pulls her hair from the ponytail, making a show out of it.

"Even when you act silly," I tell her.

"Maybe you should take a picture. It'll last longer."

"As if you'd let me. I know better."

"You're right."

I walk past her and turn on the water, allowing it to get hot as she helps me undress. Then we step inside. The warm stream pounds against my skin, and I move Summer close to me, our chests pressed together. Reaching over, she grabs a bar of soap and lathers it along my body.

I place my hand on the wall behind her, steadying myself as she uses the suds as a lubricant to easily slide over my cock.

"I didn't realize you had so many tattoos," she says, studying them.

"Yeah, they each mean somethin' to me," I explain as she strokes me. "Fuck."

My eyes are closed as she traces her lips with mine. "Feels so good."

With her other hand, she massages and washes my balls. Once I'm clean to her satisfaction, I rinse myself, and she drops to her knees.

"I want to make you feel good." She nearly begs for permission as the water pounds against my back. She studies my cock and traces the vein along the shaft with her tongue. Then she flicks against the metal ring of my piercing.

"Shit," I hiss out. "Makes it more sensitive."

"So what's this one called?" She licks around it.

"Ampallang or some shit."

Summer looks impressed, then opens her mouth wide and takes me in.

As she rests one of her palms flat on my upper thigh, she uses the other to guide me in. She licks up and down the shaft and like a very good girl, gently sucks on my balls. Then she slowly slides me into her mouth. When I touch the back of her throat, she gags.

I'd be lying if I said it wasn't the hottest fucking thing I've ever seen.

She tries again, giving it her best effort as she looks up into my eyes. Then surprising me, her free hand falls between her legs, and I watch as she sucks me off and teases her clit. "Goddamn, what a sight to see. Get yourself close, but don't you dare fuckin' come. You'll need to earn every orgasm you get tonight."

Summer blinks up at me, then shoves two of her fingers inside her pussy before returning to her needy clit. I reach down, twisting one of her nipples, and see something flash behind her eyes.

I love watching her grow desperate. She strokes and sucks me so damn good, and watching her pleasure herself is almost too much.

I can tell she's close, and if she keeps it up at this pace, I will be, too.

"Give me your hand."

She dips it inside her pussy one last time before lifting her wrist. I capture her moist fingers in my mouth, sucking them clean. Then I fist the back of her wet hair, letting her know I'm about to explode. She understands and slows to a deadly pace.

She's a vixen, a bad girl, and when I spill into her mouth, she moans, pulling away so I can see the silver strands fly into the back of her throat and land on her tongue.

"Mmm." Summer swallows me down like a good girl. She licks up every drop and drinks me down. Her hooded eyes meet mine, and I hold out my arms, lifting her to me. When our mouths crash together, our arousals mix, creating a symphony of flavors.

"You're so sexy." I search her green eyes.

"Well, get ready. Because you ain't seen nothin' yet."

17

SUMMER

*E*ven though I was pissed, I knew my answer would be yes when he asked me to come home with him. For as long as I can remember, this is what I've wanted—him and him wanting me back. I feel like I've finally peaked in life, and hey, a win is a win, even if it means I lose Horseshoe Creek Ranch in the end.

However, I'm just hoping this will show him how much he fucked me, literally and figuratively. After we get out of the shower, Beckett grabs a fluffy towel from the closet and begins drying me.

"Okay, I could get used to this."

He chuckles, touching every inch of me, then wraps the terrycloth around me and grabs one for himself. Once we're dry, he leads me into his bedroom.

A large, king-sized, hand-carved four-poster bed fills the room, along with ranch decor and old cowboy images. I glance at him. "So this is where the magic happens."

"Only when I'm thinkin' about you, sweetheart."

"Yeah, right." I don't believe him.

He shrugs. "How do I prove it to you?"

"Let me watch you."

He takes a step forward, wrapping his strong hand around my waist and pulling me to him. "That'd make you wet?"

"You have no idea." My body wants him so badly, it's more like a desperate need. I need his thick cock inside me sooner rather than later, but I'll play his games.

Beckett agrees and lies down on the bed, opening his towel and tucking one arm behind his head. I watch how his bicep flexes, studying the tattoos on his arm. Muscles cascade down his chest and stomach, creating hard lines on his body.

"Show me how you do it."

Roughly, he grabs his length, working himself. I drop my towel, lifting my breast to lick my nipple, then slide my hand between my thighs. My pussy clenches with anticipation as I barely brush my fingertips over my clit.

Beckett grunts as he strokes a little faster. "Shit, come here."

A smug grin meets my lips as I saunter over to the bed. He reaches over to pull open the drawer next to his nightstand, and I stop him.

"No. I don't want anything between us." I have a birth control implant. "I'm covered."

"You sure?" He meets my eyes.

"Yes, I want to feel you, Beck. All of you." I grab his thick dick, which is at full attention.

Gracefully, I crawl onto the bed as he watches me. I love being a specimen under his microscope, having every ounce of his attention. A part of me thinks I could get used to this, but I quickly push that thought away. Pressing my palms onto the bed, I lift my leg to straddle his lower stomach.

"You're goin' for it, baby girl." He opens his mouth, sucking on my nipple, then releases it.

"I need you to break me, Beckett." I line up the tip of his cock with my opening and slowly slide down on him.

His thumbs dig into my hips. "You're so goddamn tight,"

he hisses as I stop, allowing my body to adjust to every thick inch of him. I lower myself a bit more, little by little, until he's inside me. He fills me so full, stretching me to fit him.

"You okay?"

He rests my palms on his chest, and I think I might be split into two.

"Your cock should be illegal," I whisper. "Or in pornos."

"But instead, it's in you." He chuckles as I grind against him.

"Fuck, and it feels so good." A moan escapes me as I barely rock my hips, trying to get used to the sensation of him. "I'm pretty sure this is why you're single."

"Because my cock is too big?"

"Fuck yeah." I whip my hair back, allowing my head to fall back on my shoulders as moans escape me. I work him in and out of me, and I'm so wet for him.

Each time my pussy clenches, he cusses, grabbing my hips.

I need more of him, all of him.

Beckett places his hands firmly on my ass cheeks, adding more friction as our tongues tangle together. A sensation I've never felt before builds inside me, and we keep going harder and faster.

"I...I..." I'm at a loss for words as an orgasm builds *without* any clit play. "Shiiii—" I can't even finish the sentence before I'm coming, my pussy squeezing him tightly.

I continue to lose myself. My thighs tremble with satisfaction as I try to catch my breath. I topple on top of him, sliding my tongue into his mouth.

"I've never come that way before."

He searches my face and gives me his signature boyish grin. "Glad I could still be a first for something. Must've been hitting that G-spot."

"Or it's the dick ring. Either way, it was incredible. *Different.* I want to do it again."

He chews on his bottom lip and gives himself another stroke. "Do you always come so...*violently*?"

"Sometimes," I admit. "Especially when I edge myself to oblivion or if I'm super turned on."

"Ahh, that explains a lot." He smirks.

"Explains what? Tell me."

"Your willingness to prolong it. You enjoy holding off. Some women immediately want the orgasm."

I blush. "What's the rush, though? We've got all night."

"Exactly."

I roll over and position myself on all fours. He eyes my perfect ass and growls, then climbs off the bed. He grabs my feet, scooting me to the edge of the mattress, and I desperately need to feel him deep inside me again. I glance over my shoulder to see him grab his cock, centering himself, then tapping his head against my pussy.

Fuck, it feels so good.

"Yes, yes." I arch my back while grabbing the comforter with white knuckles. "Fuck me," I nearly beg him.

While I want him to impale me, he doesn't. Beckett takes his time and moves slowly.

After a few pumps, I moan and slam myself against him, taking in every damn inch.

"Careful, sweetheart. You still need to walk tomorrow," he warns me with a smack of my ass. I yelp; my pussy throbs, loving the pain, but I appreciate him rubbing his firm palm against my cheek.

"God, you're so fucking tight. Stretching around me like that."

I slam against him, creating more friction, loving all the places he's marking.

We're lost in each other, and when he reaches around and rubs my clit, gibberish releases from the back of my throat. He gives me every bit of him, and I feel like I've died and gone to heaven as he pleasures me in ways I'm not used to. Beckett makes sure I come again and again and again.

"Lie down, sweetheart."

I crawl up the bed and lie on my back. Beckett hovers above me with arms on either side of my head. He studies my face before dipping down and kissing me softly, full of passion. "I owed you that."

I make a face.

"Fourth of July," he whispers, deepening the kiss, swiping his tongue against mine. "I wanted to kiss you then. I was so close, but I chickened out."

"Why?"

"I got scared. I was about to be a senior, and you were going to be a freshman. The age difference felt strange. Like you were too young."

I place my palm on his cheek and smile. "I guess it didn't matter in the end, did it? Somehow, we still ended up fuckin'."

He chuckles. "Yeah, but I realize now that I hurt you."

I nod. "You *were* the first boy I cried over."

Beckett swallows hard. "I'm sorry."

"You're forgiven...for that. Other things, I'm not so sure about." I smile, meeting his soft gaze.

"Let me make it up to you."

I reach up and pinch his nipple, and the mood shifts back to playful. "Maybe."

For a moment, I see the real Beckett, the glimpse of that boy I crushed on all those years ago. The air in the room shifts when he slowly guides himself inside me.

I widen my hips, adjusting myself, wanting every part of him. He kisses me, and it's slow, intimate, with more meaning behind it than I expected. We're not having sex anymore... we're past that.

There's no rushing. It's just me and him in the moment. One that I wish could last forever, one that I'd be happy to be suspended in. One where Beckett and I are two different people who don't hate each other. Then I ask myself if I've ever really hated him, or if it's a story I've told myself to protect my heart.

My breathing increases, and his soft pants in my ear drive me wild.

I'm close, so damn close.

I scratch my nails down his back and lift my feet, pushing them into his ass. Every inch of my body tenses, and I sway on the edge. My orgasm is right there, but I wait for him to join me. When he tenses, I give myself permission and allow myself to let go. He spills inside me, our lips and bodies a tangled mess of satisfaction.

I don't think I have another ounce of energy left inside me, and Beckett doesn't seem to either. We fall back on the bed, and he pulls me into his arms. I rest my head on his chest, hearing his rapidly beating heart, and I love knowing I was the reason for that.

"Tell me about this rose tattoo on your elbow," I say.

He softly smiles. "I know it's your favorite flower. Yellow, to be exact. It reminds me of you."

I swallow hard. "Beck. You got a flower tattoo for me?"

"It felt right."

"I don't know what to say other than it's beautiful."

He smiles, his eyes closing, and eventually, I come back to reality. Physical exhaustion finds me.

"I still don't like you, and I'm still very much pissed off at you."

Then he leans over, pulls me closer, and places a soft kiss on my forehead. "Sounds like you're tryin' real hard to convince yourself of that."

"I mean it." But do I?

"I know, sweetheart. But if that's how you fuck people you don't like, maybe ya need a come-to-Jesus moment."

I laugh. "Good night, Beck."

"Night, SumSum."

He flicks off the side lamp next to his bed, and when I roll onto my side, he holds me. His breathing softens, and I ask myself how long I'll keep fighting these feelings.

Forever?

Maybe I won't win the property, but right now, there's much more at stake…like my heart.

18

BECKETT

*R*olling over, I reach for Summer and wake to an empty bed. I climb up off the mattress, put on some joggers, then make my way to the living room to see if she's up and waiting for me.

The house is empty.

She's gone.

Probably waited until I fell asleep last night, then snuck out. Well, *shit.*

Running my fingers through my hair, I go to the kitchen and make some coffee. While it's brewing, I sit at the breakfast nook trying to wake up. It's barely past six, and the sun has just started to rise. Last night, we stayed up pretty late, but I have no regrets.

I contemplate texting her, but then I remember what she said before she came home with me. Last night was possibly just sex to her, and while I won't complain, it felt different. There was a shift between us, a connection much deeper than even I anticipated. I don't want things to go back to how they were.

What I want to know is how the hell she got back to the

barn. It's not that far of a walk, but she left in the middle of the night. That's pure determination.

Once the coffee pot stops dripping, I grab a mug and fill it full. It's too hot to drink, so I get dressed as I wait for it to cool. Then I can chug it and go to work. A busy body means a busy mind, and I need the distraction right now.

By the time I roll up to the barn, the lights are on, and I can hear country music playing. I check the time again, to make sure I'm not late, and for the first time in God knows how long, Harrison is early.

Wouldn't be surprised if he didn't even go to sleep.

When I walk inside, he meets my gaze. "Goooooooooooood mooooooooooornin'."

"Fuck. Are you drunk? It's too early for all that shit."

He skips over. "How was your night with Summer?"

I glare at him. "Whatcha talkin' about?"

"Oh, you know, when I was heading home from the bar, I passed her walking from your place."

"What time?"

"'Round three."

I shake my head.

"Ah, you didn't know she left, did you?" He bursts into laughter. "She escaped ya."

"Shut the hell up!" Frustration burns within me.

He shakes his head. "I stopped and talked to her."

Every bit of my being wants to ask him what she said, but I doubt he'd tell me anyway. He enjoys this shit too much.

"Good for you."

"Aw, big brother, I know you're dying to know what she said."

"I don't care." I keep my tone flat, but even Harrison knows it's a lie.

"Wait a damn second." He pauses and lifts his hand before placing it on my forehead. "Are you lovesick?"

"Can we get to work?"

He howls. "You are! Shit! Never thought I'd see the day."

"I'm not lovesick, ya ass. I'm tired from being up late."

"Yeah, well you're actin' all mopey. She already break your heart?"

"Keep it up, and I'mma break your balls."

He chuckles. "Yeah, right. My balls are already broken from the blonde I hooked up with."

"I don't want any details." I walk to the feed room and grab buckets to divvy out the food.

"She has a best friend who's single if you're interested. They live in Alpine."

"I'm not."

"That's too bad. She's hot as fuck. Apparently, she's also into yoga. You know what that means?"

I shake my head. He's talking way too much for my liking this morning.

"She's extremely flexible. Well, if you don't want her, maybe I'll have them both. At the same time."

"Like your little dick could keep up with two women."

He lifts his brow and grabs his crotch. "This little dick has."

I hold up my hand. "I don't want to know."

"Oh yeah. Best threesome of my life. I should call them sometime. Stepsisters." He grins like he's replaying a memory.

I shovel several scoops of feed into the buckets, and Harrison and I pick them up. We carry them through the barn, pouring the grain into the troughs. Once every stall is full and the animals are munching, we clean up around the place and walk into the small office. It's big enough for a desk, a laptop, and a whiteboard, where we write down our schedule each week.

"No cancellations today. Called everyone and confirmed yesterday." Harrison plops into the chair, putting his feet up on his immaculate desk.

The schedule is packed full. We've got several trail riders, a few barrel racing lessons, and then a couple of kids after school lets out. I'm grateful.

"You know, they say the best way to get over one woman is to get on top of another."

I glare at him. "There is absolutely *nothing* to get over."

"What about Natalie? She seems into you. I ran into her at the grocery store the other day."

"She's hung up on her ex. Maybe if you talked to her, you'd know that."

"Oh, I did talk to her. She gave me her number and said we should go out sometime."

I chuckle. "Then go out with her."

"Nah, bro. I don't need a pity fuck. Right now, you do."

"Kindly fuck off and mind your own business."

He snickers. "Whatever you say."

After the horses finish eating, we round them up for our first clients. I busy myself prepping and saddling them as Harrison greets our group. I know it's going to be a long day.

"Howdy, y'all." I greet the group of twentysomethings who came from the college campus. They're wearing cheap cowboy boots and hats and blue jean shorts that show their ass. Harrison lifts a brow at me, and his smile widens.

"Mornin', ladies." He personally introduces himself one by one. They giggle and look at him with googly eyes. I give everyone my name at the same time and keep the flirting out of it. However, they're not hard on the eyes.

As I lead horses out to the front so we can go over safety, Harrison falls into step beside me. "I think we won the jackpot."

I glare at him. "Absolutely not."

"How many numbers do you think I can get? All of them?"

"I'm seriously going to fire you."

No matter how many times I threaten him, he knows it's just that. He's a hard worker and makes it fun, even if he's a pain in my ass one hundred percent of the time.

One of them calls his name, while another fights for his attention.

All I can think about is Summer. Her soft pants and moans, the sound of my name on her lips. Fuck, I'm done for, aren't I?

As Harrison gives his speech, the girls laugh in the right spots, which only inflates his ego. He gets on one of the horses and explains how to use the reins and how to hold on if there's a runaway.

He takes his time with each woman, helping her up into the saddle, asking if they're comfortable. It's not lost on me how they touch his shoulder or arm or shoot him winks.

Damn, I think my brother is a ladies' man, and it's not all bullshit. Lots of realizations today.

Soon, we're all saddled and make our way down the Sunshine Trail, which leads to the top of a ridge. During the fall, I sometimes like to come out here and watch the wildlife in the mornings. Never been much of a hunter, but it's the perfect place to spot deer.

When we stop, Harrison gives some history of the ranch. I stand off to the side, allowing him to do his thing, thankful he craves attention. Right now, I'm not in the mood. I was hoping getting in the saddle would help me clear my mind, but it's only given me more time to think.

As he continues, I pull my phone from my pocket and search for Summer's contact. I click on her name and realize I haven't texted her in *years.*

I type out something and erase it.

What the hell do I even say?

Hey, how was last night? How are you? Everything okay? Why did you leave?

I shove my phone back into my pocket, frustrated. It all sounds stupid.

By the time we make it back to the barn and the ladies have left, I still haven't thought of what to send.

"What's up?" Harrison walks over to me.

165

"What do you mean?"

"You're killin' the whole vibe. Snap out of it." He's dead-ass serious.

"I know, you're right. I just…"

"You're obviously all in your head, gazing longingly at your cell phone. Just text her."

"I was going to, but I didn't know what to say." That was hard as hell to admit.

"Be truthful. Tell her you've been thinking about her."

I tilt my head. "That's it?"

"Yeah. What else would you do? Send her a poem? Roses are red. Violets are blue. I've been in a bad mood since sleeping with you."

My face cracks into a smile. "She'll just reply with a *good*."

"A reply is a reply. Send her something, then leave your phone in the office and check it when our day is done. Because right now, whatever this is, it ain't it. She's probably thinking about you, too."

"Probably not."

He gives me a pointed look. "You both deserve to be miserable without each other. That's all I'm gonna say. When I picked her up and brought her back to her Jee—"

"Wait, you picked her up?"

"Well yeah, I wasn't gonna let her walk back to the barn in the middle of the night alone. I'd have felt bad. There are literal cougars out there and not the ones I want to fuck. The ones that will rip your head off."

I chuckle.

"Anyway, she said she needed to get home because she had a lot of shit to do today. Had to be up early to feed the animals and all that. You know how this life works, Beck. Can't be fuckin' and sleepin' all day, because duties still gotta be done. I'm sure it ain't personal, so snap the fuck outta it."

"You're right." I pull my phone out of my pocket and open

her contact again. Sucking in a deep breath, I type out a message.

Thinking about you.

I show Harrison, and he grins. "Perfect, now send that shit, throw that phone in the office, and let's get to work, please?"

And I do exactly that.

The rest of the day goes by in a blur. We're nonstop busy and barely have enough time to eat lunch. The afternoon swiftly transforms into evening, and by the time we've mucked stalls and fed the animals, I'm worn out.

"Gonna grab your phone?" Harrison reminds me as we're walking out to our trucks.

"Oh yeah, shit. Almost forgot." I make my way back to the office and grab it.

Anticipation rolls through me as I unlock it and see there's a notification on my texts. I open it up and see one from Kinsley calling me an asshole for upping my bid.

However, Summer didn't respond, and deep down, I didn't think she would.

When I make my way through the barn, Harrison is waiting for me. "Well?"

I shake my head.

He squeezes my shoulder hard. "She's just playin' hard to get. Give her time."

"Don't you think a decade and a half is plenty enough time?" I shove my phone into my pocket.

"It hasn't been that long, Beck. It's been less than twenty-four hours since your dick was inside her. That's a lot to process. You know what Mama says—patience is a virtue."

"Then she should've given me some at birth."

"It's gonna be fine. Don't give up. And tomorrow, please don't come pussyfootin' around. I'm not pullin' your slack again," he says.

"Then maybe I'll call in sick?"

He laughs. "You do, and I'm slashin' your tires. Trust me when I say it ain't even a threat."

"Yeah, yeah. See ya in the mornin'. Oh, and thanks."

"No problem. Rootin' for you."

I make my way home, and that elephant returns to sitting on my chest.

Do I regret being with Summer? No.

But I didn't expect to feel like this either.

Harrison is right. I need to snap out of it, but I don't even know where to begin.

19

SUMMER

*I*t's officially been two days since I snuck out of Beckett's house after he fell asleep. I've tried my damnedest to get him out of my head, but it's been hard. No matter how busy I stay, he lingers in the back of my mind.

Yesterday, he texted me, and I ignored it. It's better this way. Or at least that's what I keep telling myself.

I meet Kinsley for lunch at the deli on the corner, and as soon as her eyes meet mine, they light up.

"You had sex." She's smirking.

"How do you know that?" I slide into the booth in front of her.

"You're glowing. Like, damn girl, your aura is bright." She sips her sweet tea but doesn't take her eyes off me.

Two menus sit on the table, but I don't waste my time looking inside. Per usual, I already know what I want.

The server comes over and greets us. I think her name is Taylor, and she's the same age as Sterling, Kinsley's younger brother who's about to graduate from high school.

"Whatcha'll havin'?" She grins wide, setting a sweet tea down in front of me.

"Chicken Caesar wrap with fries." I take a drink and thank her.

"Tay, you know I'm havin' the same thang. Besties and twinsies."

Taylor laughs and makes her way to the counter, where she hands the cook on the other side of the window a handwritten order.

Kinsley stirs her straw, making the ice scrape the edges of the plastic cup. She meets my eyes again. "I'm waaaaaiting."

I laugh. "Why do you always want to talk about my sex life in public?"

She snorts. "Because I don't see you anywhere else! Now, spill it."

A long sigh escapes me, and I feel deflated. I'm not even sure where to start or what to say.

Kinsley makes a face as I hesitate. "Uh, that's not good."

"I know. I just…I'm afraid that I'm in too deep, and all of this is going to turn out to be a huge mistake, and I'll get hurt. Then I'm never going to be able to get over Beckett, and my life is going to suck because he's going to have my dream property and my damn heart." All of my concerns flood out of me.

"Whoa, babe. What is it that you told me on Sunday?"

"I have no idea. A lot of stuff has happened since then."

"You basically said what-ifs don't matter. All of this is nothing more than a what-if situation."

I search her face, and she continues. "The fear of falling in love is real, and it can be scary because there's so much at risk. But then again, it could all work out in the end, and you could get your happily ever after. You just don't know that's why it's a risk in the first place."

"So why didn't you become a therapist again?" I give her a small smile.

"Because it's a lot more fun writing about people's problems than solving them." She winks. "But we've got a lot to unpack here. What's the biggest hang-up you're having?"

I think about it, watching the ice melt in my tea. "I just know how Beckett is noncommittal, and I'm afraid I've become nothing more than another mark on his headboard. I feel stupid. I went to confront him about changing his bid and ended up between his sheets. How the hell does that even happen? I've asked myself that question a million times. I should've been kicking him in the crotch, not..." I don't even finish. I don't have to.

She shakes her head, but her expression is soft. "I mean, that's gotta tell ya something. You were pissed, ready to destroy his existence, and you still"—she lowers her voice—"banged him."

I cover my face. "I know. I'm so stupid! Who even does that?"

"Girl, you're not stupid. The heart and body want what they want." She taps her head. "The brain can't control everything. Sometimes ya gotta throw logical thinkin' out the door. What does Summer want?"

"I don't know. That's the problem. Once I figure that out, then I'll be able to make a decision as to what I need to do next."

"Have you talked to him?"

I shake my head. "He texted me yesterday, and I didn't respond."

Her brow furrows. "What did he say?"

"Thinking about you."

"Aw, well, that's a sweet message. You should've just sent him a smiley face or something. Instead, you ghosted him." She chuckles. "He's probably spiraling."

I give her a pointed look.

"Listen, I know my brother is a huge asshole. Huge. Gigantic, even. And at times, he's the biggest dickhead I've ever had the pleasure of being related to. But I also know he's a good person. He'd do anything to help anyone, even if they don't ask. He donates ten percent of all of the money he earns to a rescue that saves elderly horses. And he's never, *ever* looked at any woman the way he looks at you."

I swallow hard, a lump forming in the back of my throat. I take a huge swig of sweet tea, but it doesn't clear it.

"You're just sayin' that." I force out the words, thinking about the tattoo on Beckett's elbow that he got for me. The air in the room feels too thick to breathe.

"I'm not, and you know deep down that I wouldn't lie about somethin' like that."

She wouldn't.

"If I'm bein' honest, I don't know what to say, Kins. I'm scared. And I'm pissed because I want that property so bad."

"Which do you want more?"

I give her a puzzled look.

"To be with Beckett or to win the ranch?"

I sigh. "You know I can't choose between those two things. I'm conflicted, and it's making me sick. I can't sleep. He's consumed me and is always on my mind, but so is the Horseshoe Creek Ranch."

"What if you could have both?"

"Impossible." I shake my head.

"Who says? I don't believe in the impossible. Maybe you were both meant to have the property and each other? It's the link that will ultimately bring you together."

"I'm having a crisis, and you're being woo-woo. I'm going to lose everything, Kins. There isn't one scenario where I win."

"And that right there is exactly why...because you believe that shit your brain is tellin' you."

Our food arrives, and we thank Taylor in unison.

"Y'all need anything else, just holler."

We nod, and I pick up my wrap, happy for the change of subject but also knowing this conversation is far from over.

"So how was it?" She waggles her brow.

"*Oh my God*, the best I've ever had. I'll spare you the details, but honestly, your brother is what wet dreams are made from."

She nearly chokes as she chuckles, then swallows down the bite she was chewing. "And this is why I'll forever be single. I'm related to all the good men in town."

"Not true. You'll find your person." My words linger for a moment. "How's the bartender?"

A sly smile touches her lips. "He's good."

"Have you…"

"Had sex? Yes. I know it's only been a few days, but he's spontaneous. I like that about him. Have you ever just fucked in the back of a truck before?" she asks so casually, just like we're talking about the weather.

"I only ever did missionary, on the bottom, before your br—"

She holds up her hand. "I don't want to close my eyes and imagine my brother naked with you."

I burst out into laughter. "True. I guess I'll spare you…this time."

"Yesterday, he picked me up after work to drive around. Then we were going to grab some steaks to cook on the grill and just couldn't wait. Did it right there in the parking lot of the grocery store." She smiles wide, proud.

I raise my hand, and we exchange a high five.

"Honestly, a first for me. I was so scared people would notice the truck rocking or hear us, but I didn't care." She shrugs. "It was *so* good. A little hot and sweaty, but neither of us was complainin'. I surely wasn't. It was exactly what I needed after a long day."

"You're gonna have to teach me your ways."

She snickers and lowers her voice. "My brother will."

I roll my eyes. "I just don't know what to do."

Kinsley studies me. "Holy shiiiiiit. You're *actually* in love with him."

"What? *No.*"

"Now you're lyin'. I can tell when you're not tellin' the truth. I saw hearts in your eyes."

I open my mouth and close it. She's onto me, and I don't think I can deny it any longer.

"*Summer.*"

I cover my face, heat rushing through me as my heart thumps rapidly. "I don't know how I let this happen."

I finally meet her gaze, and she reaches forward and squeezes my hand. "He's in love with you, too, babe."

"What am I going to do?" My voice sounds strained and desperate, and I feel like I'm spinning, because it's not something I've ever admitted. Not to her, and not to myself.

"You're gonna go for it."

"You say that with so much confidence, but…"

"Every coin has two sides. Just have to decide whether this risk is worth the reward. Oh, and get your birth control implant removed because I'd love to have a niece or nephew to spoil."

I pick up a french fry and throw it at her. It lands in her lap, and she picks it up and eats it. "You know I'm right."

"I know, and that's the part that scares me the most."

20

BECKETT

*A*s soon as I walk into my house for lunch, my phone buzzes in my pocket. I set my keys onto the table next to the door and pull out my cell. When I see Cash's name, I answer.

"Dude, what's been going on since we last chatted?" He's huffing, and I can hear some noise in the background.

"What the hell are ya doin'?"

"I'm at the gym. On a treadmill."

I burst into laughter. "And you decide to call me in the middle of your workout?"

"It's the only time I have to myself these days." He's breathless.

"You're ridiculous."

I hear beeping and belts on the machine slowing. "So. How's everything goin'?"

"It could be better."

"Shit." Then I hear a crash. Cash cusses, and moments later, he's picking up his phone. "You know, maybe I shouldn't talk and exercise at the same time."

"Probably a smart idea. You good?"

"Yeah, yeah. Still in one piece, and my phone ain't broken…yet. But anyway."

"Well, I don't have any updates. The bidding closes soon."

"Ahh, I see. Even if it doesn't work out, I thought I might move back anyway. Ever since you planted that seed in my mind, it's just been festerin'. I'm sure I can figure it out if I take that leap of faith."

I'm grinning so wide it hurts. "That would be incredible. Would almost be like old times again."

"I told my mama, and she cried at the thought. I just miss Valentine."

"Never thought I'd hear ya say that." I chuckle.

"I know, right? Yeah. My contract ends at the end of the year. There's no way they'd let me out of it early, but when the time comes, I'm not gonna renew. It's for the best. I have enough money saved to keep me afloat and start my own practice."

"Proud of you. Damn, we're gonna have some fun."

"Hell yeah, we are. But anyway, just wanted to let ya know what I've been thinking about. You're to thank."

"Nah, man. You already knew, just didn't want to admit it."

He chuckles. "So…how's Summer?"

"She's fine, I guess."

"I take it you two aren't on speaking terms…still?"

"Somethin' like that." I hear a vehicle door slam outside, and I go to the front window to peer out the blinds.

"Hey, I gotta let ya go. I'll call you later."

"Sounds good."

I end the call, and before Kinsley knocks on the door, I open it with a cheeky grin. "What pleasure do I owe you, dear sister?"

She walks past me and lets herself in. "Cut the shit."

"Hey, what if I would've had a woman in here naked or something?"

She turns and looks at me. "I honestly doubt that,

considering the only woman you'd have naked in here is workin'."

I check the time. "Shouldn't *you* be at work?"

"I'm…" She pauses. "Doing investigative journaling at the moment."

Kinsley makes herself at home in my kitchen. She pulls out some lunch meat, cheese, and mayo, then proceeds to make a sandwich with my fancy sourdough bread. I look at her like she's lost her mind.

"Anyway. I need you to stop being so chickenshit when it comes to Summer."

"'Scuse me? I'm pretty sure you're the last person on this planet who should be giving any sort of relationship advice, considering your track record."

She points the butter knife at me, and there's still a small blob of mayo on the end that falls on the counter. "This isn't about me, so don't try to change the subject. Also, do you have any other cheese? American is gross."

"Sorry, didn't realize I needed to buy my groceries based on your specific needs." I roll my eyes. "Also, I'm kindly askin' you to mind your own damn business."

"I just need you two to stop doing this back-and-forth shit. Date and get married already. Everyone else can see you're meant to be together but the two of you. Why do you think that is?"

"One of my biggest pet peeves is when someone tries to act like a matchmaker. I'll do what I want, Kins. Your friend ain't interested. So maybe you're barkin' up the wrong tree right now and lecturin' the wrong person."

She picks up the bread and takes a big bite. "No, see, that's where you're wrong. She's just afraid you're going to break her heart. And I mean, considering you're such an asshole, it's a valid fear."

I swallow hard, not able to disagree with that. "I texted her, Kins. She didn't answer. Summer isn't interested. So I don't know what you want me to do, but I don't chase anyone. Not even her. And I'm not gonna start now."

She begins picking up all the ingredients and putting them away. I walk into the kitchen, grab her sandwich, and take a bite from the other side.

"Hey!"

"Thanks, sis." I steal another bite. "This is pretty damn good."

She gives me a death glare, then takes everything back out of the fridge to make another. "I just think that if you don't tell her how you've always felt, you're gonna lose your opportunity. She's already got a date planned with someone else tonight. Is that what you want?"

The thought of Summer being with another man infuriates me. It shouldn't. She's single. She can do whatever and whoever she wants, but I thought—I fucking thought—what we shared was special.

"With who?"

She shrugs. "Some internet dude she met on a dating app."

"Hope she has fun." I pull the pitcher of sweet tea from the fridge and pour myself a big glass. She makes herself one, too, before I return it to the top shelf.

"No, you don't. You hope she has the worst time of her life. I can see it on your face."

"And?"

I wait for her to continue, for her to say something else, but she doesn't. All she does is shrug.

"That's the stance you're gonna take, then?"

"Yeah, it is. You know, you're all worried about me breakin' Summer's heart. Have you ever thought about it bein' the other way around?"

She tilts her head and studies me for a moment. "No. And you know why I say that? Because she's been in love with you since we were kids, and yes, she's stubborn as a damn mule at times, but that one thing has never changed. That, and her wanting to open that B&B. She's pretty much convinced that she's not winning the land and has given up on it."

"Why?"

"Because she said she's tired of fighting with you and for you."

"*For* me?"

"Sometimes I want to hit you upside the head to maybe knock some common sense into you. Anyway, I don't know what your plans are tonight. But it might be in your best interest to show up at the martini bar in Alpine around nine." She gives me a smirk.

"Thank you."

We hold a silent conversation. If Kinsley thinks I should show up, I will. But if Summer wants to play dirty, we'll play.

THE DRIVE to Alpine isn't too bad. Natalie and I had dinner, and then I asked her if she wanted to go on an adventure. Of course, all she wanted to talk about the entire time was Harrison. Honestly, though, I'm happy about that. It's obvious she wants nothing more out of a relationship than sex. While she's flirty with me, I know I'm in the friend zone and fine with it.

"Have you ever been to this place before?" she asks as soon as we pull up to the large black building with dim lighting.

"Once. They have great chocolate martinis."

"Oh, my favorite."

I walk around to the other side of the truck and open the door for her. I adjust my tie and shove my hands into my pockets as she wraps her arm around mine. We enter, and jazz music floats through the bar area. It's a black-tie affair type of place, one I can't see Summer enjoying herself at. Retro lighting hangs from the high ceiling, creating a speakeasy feel. It's a fancy bar you use to impress a girl or get her to suck you off later. And I'm sorry, the only dick in Summer's sassy little mouth from now on is mine.

The room has short tables, all with tea candles flickering in the center. We're greeted as soon as we enter and escorted to the far corner. I check the time on my phone and see it's just past nine. As I glance around the room, I don't spot Summer. But she'll be here. Kinsley wouldn't lie about something like that.

We sit, and I ensure I have a good view of the entrance as we're handed black menus that feel soft like cloth. The text is written in a golden cursive, and the letters are embossed.

"This is fancy." Natalie's eyes trail down the options.

Before I can say anything, the door opens, and Summer enters wearing a knee-length black dress. The douchebag next to her looks like an accountant or something, one hundred percent not her type. She smiles over at him when he says something, but I can tell it's forced. It's the same smile she gives snotty kids and nosy old women in the grocery store.

It was the same smile she even gave me at one point.

They're led across the room, and I'm grateful when they are seated far enough away for me to watch but not be seen.

"I think I will go for that chocolate martini, but the white chocolate one." Natalie draws my attention back to her.

"Oh yeah, I'm sure it's just as good."

One of the bartenders comes over. They're all wearing three-piece vests with napkins tucked into the chest pockets. "Sir, Madam, do you know what you're having?"

Natalie orders, then I go with an old favorite. "I'd like a martini, extra dirty, extra olives."

"Great choices. I'll return soon." He makes his way behind the bar. While Natalie chats about Florida and her favorite outdoor activities, my eyes wander over to Summer. It takes everything I have not to crack a smile because she looks miserable. At one point, I even see her yawn.

My phone buzzes in my pocket, and I pull it out just as our drinks are delivered.

Are you there? Because if so, she has no clue.

I hurry and type back, apologizing to Natalie.

Yep.

She hates this dude.

I can tell. Looks like she'd rather sit on a cactus.

That made me laugh. Anyway, keep me updated.

I'm just grateful she's on my side.

"Sorry about that. You were sayin'?"

Natalie laughs. "Oh, I was just askin' about Harrison. Has he ever settled down and had a long-term relationship before?"

I shake my head. "Nah. But if he found the right woman, I think he would."

She grins. "You know, I asked him on a date."

"Did you?" I pretend I don't know she's been making passes, because we need something to talk about to fill the time. Thankfully, my brother is the topic of conversation tonight.

"Yeah, he accepted. We're supposed to be goin' out this weekend."

"That's awesome. Where to?"

"Not sure. But I'm hoping it ends in his bed."

I chuckle and grab my drink, lifting it. "Cheers to that."

She laughs.

I see Summer point toward the long hall that leads to the bathroom and stand, and I decide to take the opportunity.

"'Scuse me. Gonna head to the gentlemen's room."

Natalie gives me a nod and continues sipping on her drink. "I'm gonna order another one of these. Want one?"

"Nah, I'm good." I walk away, giving Summer enough time to turn down the hallway. Then I wait, leaning against the wall with my arms crossed.

She takes her time, probably texting my sister how much of a disaster the date is. When she finally emerges, she's surprised and then angry.

"What are you doin' here?" she whisper-hisses.

I give her a smug grin and take a step forward. I don't respond, sliding my lips against hers. Her tongue darts out, massaging mine, and she moans against me.

"You shouldn't be here," she says when she pulls away. "I'm on a date."

"You should be on a date with me."

Her brow furrows. "And you should mind your own business. How did you even know I was here?" As soon as the question leaves her mouth, her eyes widen. "Kins is in trouble."

I rest my hand on her waist, looking into her eyes. "You think I'm gonna let you go out with another man?"

"You don't control me, Beckett."

I smirk. "I saw you yawning. I bet you're having a great-ass time with Mr. Accountant out there."

"He's a lawyer!"

"Same difference. That's who you could see yourself climbing into bed with every night?"

"It doesn't matter, does it?"

"Yeah, it fuckin' does. I texted you, and you didn't even reply. You haven't tried to talk to me. Is this a game to you?"

Her mouth turns into a tight line. "I told you from the beginning that sex changes nothing between us. Who are you, even? Not the Beckett who fucks women and forgets about them. This isn't the Beckett I know."

I lean and whisper in her ear, "Then I guess you've never known who I am."

She shakes her head, her heartbeat pulsing hard in her neck.

"If that's the kinda guy who does it for you, then—"

"Maybe he does."

I sarcastically laugh. "Right. You think he's going to eat that cunt like dessert?" I run my hand down her waist and up her dress, then press against her clit. She sucks in air. "You think he can make you come until you're trembling?"

I rub a circle, knowing that someone else could walk down that hall and see us at any minute. She latches onto my arm as I dip two digits inside her pussy, which is slick with desire. "Be my goddamn guest."

I pull away and place my fingers into my mouth before slamming my lips against hers. Then I walk away, not giving her a second glance. She needs to know how pissed I am. Because right now, she's the only woman I want in the world, and she's out with another man.

21

SUMMER

When Beckett walks away, I go back to the bathroom, pull my phone from the pocket in my dress, and call Kinsley.

"What the actual fuck?"

She laughs, then plays dumb. "Huh?"

"You told him where I am?"

"Yeah." She doesn't even try to deny it. "You're the one who said you were having a shitty time, not me. Thought I'd help spice it up a bit."

"Kins. He just confronted me. He's livid."

"What else is new?"

Moments later, I hear the door of the bathroom open and close, and when I turn around, I see Beckett.

"Gotta let you go," I tell Kinsley, shoving the phone into my pocket.

"What are you doin' in here?"

Beckett locks the door. "Actually, I'm not fuckin' done."

Before I can say anything, he's moving toward me like he's on a mission. His mouth attacks mine, and he hikes up my skirt. I undo his belt and his pants, and I grab his hard, throbbing cock. With force, he rips my tiny panties from my body, causing

184

me to yelp, but I don't care. He can have them, just like the others.

"Fuck, I still hate you," I mutter between breathless kisses. "But I need you like I need air."

"I knew you were gonna say that." He lifts me and sets me on the counter. This bathroom is clean, but honestly, I don't care anyway. I open my legs wide, and he impales me, nearly bursting me open.

"I hate the fact you're with someone else," he growls, pounding into me. "I hate that you didn't text me back."

He covers my mouth as I moan. "I hate that I want you so goddamn much, and you don't give two shits."

I groan, my pants and moans mixing with the ecstasy of him. I'm so fucking wet, and my pussy already aches for more.

"You drive me crazy," he admits, pumping into me hard. He holds my thighs wide, our bodies clapping together as our mouths wage war. I have no words. I have nothing to say or to think.

I'm close, so fucking close, and I know he is too. "I hate everything about you."

He takes me off the counter and twists me around. My palms are flat against it as he wraps my hair around his fist, forcing me to look into the mirror at him. I'm bent over with my back arched, ass in the air, waiting for him to enter me.

"Say it again. And mean it this time." He slams back into me.

My eyes close tight as my cunt throbs. "I hate you."

The orgasm teeters as he reaches around and pinches my nipples. The pain courses through me as he pounds into me from behind. Our bodies clap together, the sounds of our feral fucking echoing off the walls.

"I hate that..." Nothing else comes except my body.

It's an earth-shattering orgasm, one that shakes through me as Beckett grunts and spills inside me.

He leans in, squeezing my breast, the warmth of him filling

me. He whispers in my ear, "Remember who owns that pussy, Summer. Whose cum is deep inside you when you go back to that fuckin' dweeb."

He sucks on my earlobe before adjusting his cock and zipping his pants. Then just like that, he's unlocking the door and gone. I hurry and go into a stall, pantyless, and clean myself up. I can barely breathe as I try to compose myself. The truth is, I don't hate Beckett. I just dislike how my body responds to him, begs for him, even desperately *craves* him.

Once I've fully come down from my high, I try to fix my hair, then return to Clint, who's playing a game on his phone.

"You okay?" He searches my face as I look around the room, trying to spot Beckett. My eyes wander over every table, every person sitting at the bar, and he's not here.

"Would you mind if we left? I'm not feeling like myself."

"Sure, that'd be fine. I'm gettin' kinda tired anyway." When the bartender comes over, Clint pays our tab, then escorts me to his truck.

The drive back to the ranch is awkward. I squeeze my legs together, my sex aching for more of Beckett. I'm still shocked by what happened. I'd do it again, considering I knew the moment I met Clint tonight I would absolutely not be having sex with him.

As much as I hate to admit it, Beckett is right.

While Clint is a nice guy, and he's rich, he's not my type.

Soon, he's pulling into the entrance of my parents' place, then driving down the long gravel road that leads to my place.

"Would you like me to walk you in?"

I smile at him. "No, thanks."

"Okay. Have a good night." He leans over to kiss me, and I move my head so his lips press against my cheek. The last thing I want to do is give him the wrong impression, especially when I already have enough man trouble.

I get out of the truck and wave goodbye before going inside.

I lock the door, lean against it, then close my eyes, replaying exactly what happened.

Maybe I should've texted Beckett back. Perhaps I should've made an effort, but all of this is new to me.

The light hint of the perfume I'm wearing mixes with Beckett's cologne. The smell of him is on me, and I need to take a shower to clear my mind. Peeling off my dress, I make my way to the bathroom. I continue undressing, then stand under the hot stream, allowing it to pound against my skin.

After a few minutes, I grab a loofah and bodywash and clean between my legs. My pussy is already sore from having him, but I greedily want more. My heart and my head are at war with each other, and I don't know which will win. I guess when it's confirmed that I've lost the Horseshoe Creek Ranch, it will officially be over.

That part of my life that's completely consumed me for weeks won't matter anymore, and then I'll be able to move on.

After my dreams shatter, then I'll think about Beckett and me. The best thing I can do for now is to continue with my life as it is. I'll need some time to process it all. The water turns cold, so I get out and go to my bedroom. I slip on a pair of sleep shorts and a tank top, then grab my phone to text Kinsley. It's one of our things—to let the other know we're safe after dates with strangers.

I'm home. Going to bed.

Alone?

Yes.

Where's Beckett?

No idea.

I leave out *all* details as they brew in my mind. A part of me wants to thank her, while the other half wants to cuss her ass out for telling him I went on a date. But I know she means well.

Once I turn off all the lights in my house, I crawl under the sheets and try to fall asleep. My mind keeps wandering to Beckett and how good he felt buried deep inside me and how desperate his kisses were. I want to send him a text, but right now, the best thing I can do is bide my time just a little while longer.

It's obvious that things will never go back to how they were. The very last thing I had planned this year was to get my heart broken. Losing that property will destroy me enough.

A WEEK PASSES, and I don't hear from Beckett once. Kinsley hasn't mentioned his name, either. It's somewhat disheartening, considering he busted into my date like a caveman claiming me in the bathroom like I was his, then crickets. The man is more confusing than calculus.

I've purposely made trips to town with hopes of running into him. When I didn't want to see him, he'd randomly pop up. Now? It's like he's avoiding me.

Yesterday, when I ran into Harrison at the grocery store, he didn't say anything about his brother. He was his flirty self per usual and asked me when we were going on a date, to which I replied, *never*. It's as if everyone pretends Beckett doesn't exist, and I'm too stubborn to mention his name. But damn, have I wanted to. I miss him like rain in the desert.

The day passes by quickly, and by the time I make it home, I'm pretty tired.

Regardless, I take a few moments to grab the water pail that I leave by my front door, then take care of my plants. They look as desperate as I feel.

"Drink up, little buddies." I wonder if the wilted flowers are getting too much sun. I stack them on the railing of my porch, hoping it will revive them.

Just as I open the door to my place, I get a phone call from an unknown number.

"Hello?"

"Hi, Summer. It's Natalie. I just wanted to give you an update now that all the final offers have been submitted."

I swallow hard, a lump the size of Texas forming in my throat, and we all know everything is bigger here.

"Yes?" I wait impatiently for her to continue, and while she only takes a few seconds to compile her thoughts, it feels like an eternity passes.

"You didn't have the highest bid."

I knew this would be the case but didn't expect to feel this gutted. I've tried to prepare for this moment, but it didn't work. Her confirmation is a sucker punch straight to the stomach. It takes everything to hold it together and not burst into tears.

"Okay." I recognize the dream is over. "Thank you."

"However…" she continues.

I swallow back the tears, ready to hang up, ready to sit in the tub with a glass of wine and feel sorry for myself until the water turns cold.

"You *did* win."

My brow furrows. "What?"

"The highest bidder decided to withdraw before close. The property is yours. We can sign the paperwork on Monday and start the process to finalize as soon as possible."

My ears ring, and my eyes go wide. I think I'm in shock.

"Hello? Did I lose you? This damn service…" Natalie sounds annoyed.

I clear my throat. "Uh. I'm still here. Sorry."

"Are you available on Monday?"

"Yes, yes. Absolutely."

"I'll text you when my grandma and grandpa can meet up. If that's okay?"

"Yeah, that's great. Thank you."

"You're welcome. Congratulations."

Then she hangs up, and I stand there staring at the wall. I should be happy. I should be celebrating, but I can't.

Why would Beckett do this?

I didn't want to owe him anything. I wanted to win fairly. He had plans for this property, plans to open a training facility so he could expand his business. Why the hell would he give that up for me? Why?

Swallowing down my annoyance, I grab the keys to my Jeep and head over to the Bar V Ranch. I pull up to his house and notice his truck isn't there. For propriety's sake, I still get out and knock on the door, but no one answers. So I stop by the barn. I still don't see Beckett's truck, but sometimes he'll park it at his parents' house and ride a four-wheeler around.

I enter. "Hello?"

Moments later, I make eye contact with Harrison, who gives me his signature cheeky smirk. He's carrying a western saddle by the horn and a teal saddle blanket.

"Finally came to give me that date I've been beggin' ya for?"

I roll my eyes. "Where's your brother?"

"Which one? I have *four*. Twenty-five percent chance of getting it right."

"You *know* which one," I say between gritted teeth.

"Sterling? I think he's at home. But I'm not sure what you'd want with an eighteen-year-old."

He's testing me, and instead of being funny, it only infuriates me. But then again, that's Harrison.

"Beckett." I'm losing my cool.

"Oh, *that* brother. You should've just said my *older* brother. Would've narrowed it down for me." He pretends to be deep in thought, and I follow him into the tack room. He takes his time setting the gear onto the saddle horse.

"I'm going to kick your ass," I warn, but I'm serious.

He chuckles, finding my agitation a little too amusing. "I *think* he went horseback riding."

I pull my phone from my pocket. "It's after six."

Harrison shrugs. "Is there a cutoff time?"

"I need a horse." I grab a bridle off the wall and make my way into the pasture.

"You can't do that." He quickly follows me. "Summer. Don't be a horse thief."

"Kindly fuck off, Harrison." There's venom in my tone. "I'm goin' searchin' for your brother because I got a bone to pick with him."

"You want to bone him?"

My nostrils flare as I grab a beautiful white paint horse with big red spots. She'll do. I grab her halter, then easily slide the bit of bridle into her mouth and slip the leather behind her ears. Then I look around and notice a tree stump by the fence.

"What are you gonna do, ride bareback?"

"Yeah. So?"

He shakes his head. "You're gonna kill him, aren't you?"

"I might." I grab a boost from the stump and slide right on.

"Also, have fun with that one. Her name is Spitfire for a reason."

"Are you talking to me or the horse?" I click my heels and take off through the barn.

I haven't ridden bareback since I was much younger, but this is how I learned. Tomorrow, I'll be sore as fuck, but right now, it doesn't even matter. Finding Beckett is the only thing that does, and if he is anywhere, it's on this trail. It's been one of his favorites for as long as I can remember. After our first official date, it's special to me, too.

Spitfire gallops fast like the wind, and I squeeze my thighs tight, holding on. The reins are light in one hand as I keep my arms close to my body. Right now, we're as one, traveling down a double-track trail that seems like a never-ending labyrinth of twists and turns. Leaves rustle on the branches as the sun hangs lazily in the distance. The crickets have come up to play their evening symphony for those who will listen. I have a few hours before the sun fully sets and the stars come out, so I need to find him immediately.

I don't even know what I'll say when I'm face-to-face with him. *If* that happens. Owning the Horseshoe Creek Ranch is what I wanted, but not like this. I'm conflicted, and my issues with this are rooted deep inside.

As I'm lost in thought, a brown-colored rabbit hops onto the trail, and Spitfire nearly loses her shit, rearing up and side-stepping like she's never seen an animal so small. It almost takes me by surprise, but considering I've broken several of the horses on my family's ranch, I handle it without falling, which is honestly a small miracle without stirrups to hold me in.

My heart races, and I decide to take it at a normal pace the rest of the way. But we're close. I can see the clearing in the distance and the water rippling in the pond.

When I make it to the end, Beckett's sitting on a log, side-tossing pebbles into the water. Ripples build and travel across the surface. I was never very good at that.

"What're ya doin' here?" He doesn't even turn around to look at me, like he expected me to come. Maybe he did.

I slide off Spitfire, tie her to the post next to where Beckett's horse stands, then walk over to him.

"I want to know the same thing." I place my hands on my hips. It's the first time I've seen him since the night at the martini bar. He finally turns, looking at me over his shoulder. His blue eyes pierce straight through me, causing my heart to lurch forward.

"If you're so inclined to know, I'm out here clearin' my mind."

I take a few steps forward. "Why did you withdraw your bid? That's the stupidest thing you've ever done."

He pats the log he's sitting on, and I join him but leave space between us. Nonchalantly, he picks up another rock and tosses it across the pond. It skips four times before sinking to the bottom.

"Are you gonna tell me why you did that?" The silence draws on for way too long.

"Are you mad?" He glances over at me.

"Yes and no." I suck in a deep breath. "I just don't understand you. One minute you're hot, the next minute you're cold, then the very next week you—"

Beckett's lips slam against mine, his fingers running through my hair. I moan against him, needing this more than I even knew. I'm greedy and breathless, and while I want to push him away, I also want to drink in his taste, his touch, his smell. All of him.

"You know why I pulled my bid?" He pulls away, trailing kisses from my lips to my ear. "Because I've fallen for you, Summer."

My breath grows unsteady, my heart ready to explode. "And I want you to be happy. I know, if you'd give me the chance, I could make you the happiest woman alive. But I also don't know if you're ready for that. So giving up Horseshoe Creek Ranch was the next best thing. It's my gift to you. I want you to be happy. I want all your dreams to come true." He searches my face.

I place my hand on his cheek as I meet his soft eyes.

"I didn't want your charity, Beck."

He swallows hard. "I understand if this was all a game to win the property. If this meant nothing to you, I need to know so I can move on. So I can stop waitin' around. So I can go back to hatin' the fact that I can't have you."

"You didn't let me finish. I didn't want your charity. I just want you. And only you." I wrap my arms around his neck and devour his lips, our tongues twisting together to the sound of the crickets chirping.

"It was never a game," I admit.

"I've only ever wanted you, Summer."

His admission has my emotions bubbling as heat rushes through my body. He unravels me with just one look before our lips crash together. His tongue dips into my mouth, twisting and tangling with mine, and one thing is for certain—I want him, I *need* him, *right fucking now.*

22

BECKETT

*S*ummer stands and straddles me, wrapping her arms around my neck. My cock is hard, and she roughly rocks against me, like she enjoys the friction of me through my jeans.

"I have to know what this means, Summer." I grab her ass with my palms and meet her eyes. I can't continue to fuck without feelings. It's not just sex with her. It never was. "Will you give us a chance?"

"Yes, yes," she desperately whispers. "If you want me, I'm yours, Beck. I've always been."

"That's all you had to say, sweetheart."

Summer removes her shirt and sets it on the log. The anticipation of being one again drives us forward. I kiss the tops of her supple breasts, which are nearly falling out of her bra, then slide my hand under the fabric to tweak her perky nipple. Her moan only urges me to continue, so I give the other a firm twist.

"You've always known what I like." She reaches behind her and unsnaps her bra. It falls between us, and I place it on top of her shirt before leaning forward and taking her hard little peak into my mouth.

I twist my tongue around one nipple, then switch to the other, giving them equal play.

Her breathing grows ragged as she rocks her hips. Having her like this, tasting her, kissing her, smelling her…knowing we're going to be together is a heady combination. I'm on a high, and it feels like I'm living in one of my dreams where she's mine, except this is my new reality.

"I need you so damn bad," she urges with a desperate look in her eyes, reaching down to unbutton and unzip my jeans.

Sparks fly between us, and together we're electric.

Summer stands, sliding off her boots, jeans, and panties. She's eager, and when I reach forward to touch her, I realize she's dripping fucking wet. As always.

"My eager girl." I thumb her clit, then stand and give her full access to me.

My cock is at full attention as I sit back, and she slides on top of me in one swift movement. Her walls are tight, and her pussy clenches hard around me, causing me to groan with satisfaction.

Our breaths are uneven and ragged as I give her complete control to take whatever she needs. I'm hers, after all, and her pussy devours me from tip to base over and over, making me damn near powerless. We kiss, and I thread my fingers through her dark hair, unable to get enough of her.

"Beck," she whispers in a hushed tone. Our low grunts fill the space as we rush toward the finish line, a race we'll continue to run together for as long as she allows. I'm hers, and she's mine. The way it's always meant to be.

I kiss down the corner of her mouth, down her jaw, and squeeze one of her perfect tits while sucking the other.

"You're so fuckin' beautiful." I mean every last word.

Her head falls back on her shoulders as she takes every fucking inch of me, rough and then soft. Fast then slow.

"This is what I've always wanted." She moans, thrashing

her fingers through my hair and tugging as her tight cunt greedily devours my cock. "You. Just like this."

"Forever."

Her hazy eyes flutter open, and her movements slow as she rests her arms on my shoulders. "Please don't break my heart."

I press my palms against her cheeks, studying her as I'm balls-deep inside her. "I only plan to break this sweet cunt."

"Fuck yes." She kisses me and rocks against me.

I reach down, rubbing circles against her needy little clit with my thumb. "I'm yours, SumSum."

She bounces on my cock, and I fucking love the sounds of her ass clapping against my thighs.

"I'm so close," she whispers. "So damn close."

"Me too, baby. Take what you need, but turn around."

She bites the corner of her lip and smirks. "Reverse cowgirl?"

"My favorite fucking position."

"I've never…"

"You'll love it."

Summer stands, and I move to the grass and lie down. She turns, giving me the best view of her perfect ass, then slides onto me backward.

She trembles and sighs, her back arching once I'm fully inside her.

"Fuck. You're so deep. It…feels…so…"

She rests her palms on my thighs, and I trail my fingers down her back.

"I'm going to try something, sweetheart. You trust me?"

She looks at me over her shoulder and nods. I know she's so damn close, I can smell her arousal. I dip my finger between her legs, capturing some of her precum, before sliding my finger into her tight ass.

She sighs.

"Relax, sweetheart," I say in a husky tone. "How's that?"

"It feels so good," she admits, and I can tell she's about to spill over. I curl my finger in her ass when she picks up her pace.

"Fuck." Her thighs shake, and her whole body begs for release. "I love your cock."

I chuckle as she continues chasing her pleasure, bucking on me. I grab her ass with my free hand, creating more friction as she slams down on me. Her moans echo through the trees, and soon she's tipping over the edge, losing herself.

I groan. Her pussy is like a vise, squeezing me so damn hard that I can't hold back any longer. She continues to ride out her release as I spill deep inside her, giving her every drop of my hot cum.

I hold her tight against my body. Her skin is sticky with sweat. She slides off me and lies beside me in the grass, resting her head against my shoulder. I hold her naked body and listen to the crickets chirp as the sun sets.

"It's never felt like that before." She traces the outline of the rose tattoo.

I meet her hooded gaze. "It's how I knew."

"Knew what?" she breathlessly asks, running her hand across my stomach.

"That we were made for each other."

She smiles. "That's when?"

I give her a wide smile. "Yeah."

"I knew Fourth of July all those years ago."

"Come home with me? I want to make you dinner, have you for dinner, and then wake up with you in my arms."

She grins. "I'd love that. However, I'm not sure I can bareback it all the way to the barn after that."

I let out a howl of laughter. "You didn't saddle up?"

"No, I was mad. I stole a horse from your brother and came straight here."

I shake my head. "Why were you mad?"

She gives me her signature scowl. "Because I know how much that property meant to you and Harrison."

"And Cash."

"Cash?"

"Yeah, I told him I'd lease him a piece to build his private practice."

She shakes her head and sits up. I can't help but stare at her gorgeous tits. "My face is up here."

"You can't blame me, though, you little temptress."

She gives me a small smile. "Can we compromise?"

I search her face, resting my hand behind my head. "I'm listenin'."

"Let's share the property. We can write up a contract and all of that just in case we don't work out—"

I interrupt her. "I'm not going anywhere."

"I get that, but people don't get married with the intention of gettin' a divorce."

"That's a promise, Summer. But if you want the paperwork signed, I'm fine with it. If that's what you want. Don't worry about us. We'll figure it out."

She leans forward and kisses me. "I want your dreams to come true, too."

"They already have." I slide my lips across hers.

"We can both win, Beck. We both make that property work for us." She smiles, then playfully rolls her eyes. "And I guess Cash and Harrison, too. There's enough acreage for us to do all the things. All of it will help Valentine."

I shake my head with a grin and softly brush the back of my fingers against her cheek. "And this is why you're incredible."

"Why?"

I trace my lips against hers before kissing her again.

"Because you think about everyone and not just yourself. Thank you."

"This is all because of you being selfless, not me." She struts over to her clothes and gets dressed.

"I just wanted the best for you."

"And I want the best for you. Now, Cowboy, take me home."

"Happily."

I pick her up and carry her in my arms, and she squeals with laughter. "Not like that!"

"You're light." I set her down beside my horse. "This is Magnolia. She's a sweetheart." Then I see who she rode. "Spitfire?"

She tilts her head, giving me a puzzled look. "Yeah, why?"

"She's not even fully trained. You could've gotten hurt."

Summer shrugs, but I can tell she's slightly annoyed. "She did great. Also, fuck Harrison for not telling me that."

"He probably thought you could handle it, which you did."

She puts her foot into the stirrup and climbs on. I untie Spitfire, then grab the reins.

"You ridin' bareback?"

"Hell no. I'm hopping up there with you, and we'll lead her back. I ain't gettin' fucked up tonight."

Summer slips her foot out of the stirrup giving me room to climb on. I kiss her neck before settling behind her, then we ride to the barn with my chest pressed against her back. I inhale her sweet scent and trail kisses along her neck and ear every chance I get.

"Sun is setting," I whisper.

"Mmm, the closure to a perfect day." Her voice is light and airy, and I know she means it.

When we arrive at the barn, Harrison waits with a big-ass grin on his face.

"You two fuck it out?"

"Shut the hell up." I slide off the back, then lead Spitfire to the pasture. I remove the halter and let her go. When I return, Summer is removing the saddle from Magnolia. I take it from her hands and put it away.

"So I guess I'm not ever gonna get that date, am I?" Harrison pretends to pout, but I see his smirk.

"Back off my woman," I say.

Summer beams.

"Oh, she's your woman now? You two official?"

"Hell yeah, we are." Summer wraps her hand around the back of my neck and pulls me into a kiss. It grows heated, and she hops up, straddling me as I hold her up by her ass.

"Geez. I didn't ask for a show."

I pull away, glancing at him. "Fuck off." Then I deepen the kiss.

"Happy for you two. Also happy I knew before Kinsley." He shrugs.

Summer breaks away, and her eyes go wide. "Oh goodness, she's gonna be pissed that Harrison knew first."

"You didn't tell her your intentions before you stole that horse?" I search her face.

Summer shakes her head. "I didn't even tell her about winning the ranch."

"You are fuuuucked." Harrison slaps his hand on his thigh as Summer has a complete meltdown.

"Shit." Summer pulls her phone from her back pocket. "I gotta text her right now, or she's going to write me off!"

"She'll be fine, because Harrison ain't gonna say shit."

"Says who?" Harrison fires back.

"Says me." I lift a brow. "Don't start nothin'."

"You know the magic word," Harrison says.

"Don't make me kick your ass."

He shakes his legs together. "I'm soooo scared I'm tremblin' in my boots. Tell me what I want to hear, and my lips will be zipped."

Harrison waits with lifted brows as Summer feverishly types on her phone. I can only imagine what my sister is saying right now.

"I'm waiting," he sing-songs, finding delight in my agitation.

I huff. "I'll do your weekend feedings next week."

He shakes his head. "Next *month*."

"That's not fair. Half the month."

Summer glares at me and gives me a stern look.

"Fine."

"I already like her a lot. Thanks, bro. Lips sealed." He pretends to lock his mouth and throws away the key.

He takes a step forward, leaning in, and whispers, "Happy for you."

"Thanks, asshole," I mumble, but then I laugh.

Summer finishes her conversation with Kinsley, and my phone immediately starts blowing up with texts. One thing about my sister, she wastes zero time.

"Go ahead," Summer says.

I sigh, unlocking my phone to seventeen text messages from Kinsley. I scroll down and read the very last one.

> So when's the wedding? Because that's when you're getting your TOLD YOU SO!

All I can do is shake my head, then I turn to Harrison. "Those pretty lips of yours better stay sealed."

"Scout's honor."

I glance at Summer. "You ready to get outta here?"

"Yeah. But one thing—where's your truck?"

"At my parents'."

"Ah, I figured so." She reaches out and grabs my hand, interlocking her fingers with mine. "I'll drive."

"Have fun, lovebirds," Harrison yells as we leave the barn.

The Jeep is unlocked, and I climb inside. The top is removed, and the sun has set below the hill. Alan Jackson plays in the background, and I can't help but smile as her hair flies all around. I look over at her, drinking her in, wanting to capture how beautiful she is in my memory forever.

She glances at me. "What?"

"Nothin'." I reach over and grab her hand as she drives.

"You're thinkin' about somethin'. Tell me." She takes her focus from the road and glances over at me, wearing a grin.

"I love you." I speak those words with my full chest.

She comes to a stop in the middle of the gravel road. Summer turns to me, placing her palm on my cheek. "I love you, too, Beck. I always have."

I trail my fingertips across her cheek and softly kiss her. "I'm never letting you go, SumSum."

"Don't make promises you can't keep." She smiles, and I kiss her nose.

"It's not a promise, sweetheart. It's a fuckin' fact. Now let's go. I've got a lot of provin' to do."

She hums. "I love the sound of that."

"Wait until my face is buried deep in your cunt."

As soon as the words leave my mouth, she presses on the gas like her life depends on it. Gravel and dust are thrown up in our wake, and by the time we make it to my place, we're ready for round two.

"You got any plans tomorrow?" I pop a brow, interlocking my fingers with hers, guiding her up the steps.

"Bein' with you."

"Love the fuckin' sound of that." I lead her into the house, push her against the door, and crash my lips against hers.

She's desperate and needy as she unzips my jeans and pushes my boxers down. Before I can say anything, she's on her knees. "Mmm. I can taste us on you."

I fist her hair, my eyes firmly locked on hers. She works me so damn good, and my head falls back against the door.

"What's your O record?" She pops her lips around the tip of my cock, licks the precum off the tip, and watches the sticky strands snap.

"Uh, you've already beat it, sweetheart."

Her eyes go wide.

I lift her chin up, forcing her to look into my eyes. "No other woman has ever meant as much to me as you, Summer.

I've spent my whole life waitin' for my perfect woman to realize the perfect man was always right in front of her."

"Oh, whatever. I've been waiting for you for as long as I can remember."

I laugh. "We're both too stubborn for our own good."

She leans forward, opening her mouth and sucking on my balls. I groan.

"You were sayin'?" She's wearing a mischievous grin.

"Fuck, I love you so damn much. I'm pissed at myself for waitin' so long."

She takes my cock into her mouth and forces me to the back of her throat.

"Careful, baby. Don't want that pretty little mouth of yours to be sore."

She uses one hand, twisting and tugging at my cock as it throbs for her. The other hand reaches around and grabs a handful of my ass.

"Shit." I grunt, my breathing increasing, my heart rate ticking upward.

She pulls away, continuing to work me with her hand. "Give me your cum, Beck. Fuck my mouth."

"That's what you want?"

She opens wide.

"Take off your shirt. I want to see your beautiful tits."

She does but then also completely undresses.

"I'm a goner." My cock begs to impale her. But she drops to her knees again, and I let her lead the way.

She digs her fingers into my ass, wanting me to thrust my hips forward, so I give her exactly that. I fuck her wet, hot mouth as she reaches up and pinches my nipples. She tweaks them so damn good that I won't be able to hold back any longer.

"Oh, Sum—" I can't finish what I was saying, because the orgasm shatters through me. My knees nearly buckle, and my vision blurs. She milks me dry, sucking down every drop of my cum.

"Mm." She licks her lips, biting down on the bottom one. "And just think, that was only the appetizer."

She stands and kisses me, and I can taste the saltiness of myself on her tongue.

"You know." I slide my lips across hers, not adding any pressure. "I only have one regret."

"Yeah?" Her hushed tone is serious.

"Not pursuing you earlier."

She smiles against my mouth. "True, but at least we found our way to each other in the end."

I lift her, and her legs instinctively wrap around my waist as I slide deep inside her. She writhes against me, holding on to me for dear life as I carry her to the bathroom.

"First, we shower. Then I'll eat you. Make you dinner. Fuck your brains out all night, then we'll have breakfast and do it all again."

"Sounds like a plan." She holds back a smile.

"What's that look for? You don't think you can handle it?" My brow is popped as I watch her.

"Handle it? *Bless your heart.* That's cute." Her expression turns from sarcastic to devious. "By the morning, I'm gonna own your cock."

I chuckle and kiss her, pumping into her a few times. "Babe, you already do."

23

SUMMER

"Yikes." Beckett glances at the dead flowers surrounding the house I'm transforming into the bed-and-breakfast. He runs his fingers through his messy hair and looks over at me. "You sure about this?"

The house was painted last week, and it's all starting to come together. His brother Colt is helping me remodel, and we'll officially be able to open in about six weeks. "I want to try to landscape the place myself."

I can tell he's holding back laughter by the smug grin on his face. "It's not a *great* idea."

"Listen, give me a month. If it still looks like shit before the grand opening, I'll hire someone."

Beckett holds out his hand. "Shake on it."

I glance down at his palm and then begrudgingly take it. "Fine. Deal. But I'm not givin' up hope yet. I know I can do this."

"Listen, I love ya to the moon and back, and I appreciate your willingness to do this yourself. But keepin' a bunch of plants alive for longer than a week ain't one of your strengths, SumSum."

I push out my bottom lip, trying to pout even though I

know he's right. "Out of all the people in Valentine, you should believe in me."

"I do. I believe you're gonna kill every single flower you put into the ground. Listen, Vera can help you. She's incredibly talented and would probably do it on the side for cheap. The girl could grow flowers in hell."

I playfully roll my eyes. "Well, why couldn't we all be so lucky?"

"Have you tried succulents?"

I cross my arms over my chest. "I've tried *everything*."

His mouth falls open. "How does a person kill a cactus?"

"Good question. Vera wasn't convinced I'd keep it alive either, and you know what? She was right."

Beckett chuckles, wrapping an arm around my shoulders as we stare at the decaying plants I put into the soil right after we signed the paperwork. "You're the most adorable plant murderer I've ever met."

"And now I'm even more determined to prove you wrong."

He brings me in and kisses my forehead. "I hope you do, but you got a long-ass way to go."

"Hush."

His brows rise. "I look forward to properly delivering you a Valentine Told Ya So when Vera is landscapin' the place."

I slide my lips across his. "Can you deliver that message buried deep between my legs?"

Beckett tugs on my bottom lip with his teeth and sucks. "Every damn day of the week."

My cell phone buzzes in my pocket and interrupts the moment.

"Don't answer it," Beckett says right before he slides his tongue into my mouth.

I pull it from my back pocket and lift it so I can see who's calling while I kiss him. It's Kinsley.

I answer, putting her on speakerphone. Beckett playfully rolls his eyes.

"Are you busy fuckin' my brother?"

"Not yet." He smirks. "What's up?"

"I just heard the funniest story of my life."

"Yeah?"

Beckett takes a step forward, his hand sliding into my leggings. As soon as he touches my clit, I don't hear a word Kinsley says.

She's talking about a goat. Or a cow. Or both? Shit. Is it a bird? I don't know, and I can't focus on anything else but Beckett. The story lasts a few minutes, and she can barely talk she's laughing so hard.

When she finishes, she clears her throat. "Isn't that hilarious?"

My mouth is open, and my eyes are closed. I don't think I can form words, but I force laughter. "Yeah, that's so funny."

The line is silent for a few seconds.

"You didn't hear anything I said, did you?"

"Sure."

Kinsley groans. "You're so lying! Okay, well, I'm gonna let you get back to doing whatever you're doing...*Beckett!*"

"Love you, sis." He speaks loudly so she can hear him.

"I manifested your entire relationship! I manifested you sharing the ranch, and this is my repayment? That was some hard work."

Beckett and I meet each other's eyes and burst into laughter.

"Ugh. I hate y'all! So cute and lovey-dovey. Meanwhile, I'm gonna end up an old maid!"

"Oh hush, no, you're not," I say.

"I am. Do not get pregnant until I say. That's a demand. I want our kids to grow up together."

"Okay, deal."

"Whoa, now." Beckett takes the phone from my hand. "Kins, no. You don't get to dictate our baby situation."

She tells him to shut up and mind his own business.

Beckett scoffs. "I don't care if you two were friends first. You're not the one who's going to marry her."

Heat rushes to my cheeks. The thought of marrying Beckett has been on my mind a lot lately because I can't imagine myself with any other man.

"Okay, y'all." I take my phone back from him. "I'm super flattered that y'all are fightin' over me, but honestly, it's not necessary."

"You're mine." They say it in unison.

"Maybe y'all should water balloon fight it out?"

Beckett's fingers are pressed against my clit, and when he pushes two digits inside, I cover my mouth with my spare hand. I sink onto his touch, greedy for him. He makes me so damn horny I can barely take it.

"Okay, when?" Kinsley sounds serious.

"Geez, I was kidding. Play nice. There's enough of me to share." Beckett pops a third finger into my wet hole. My pussy aches for all of him. I let out a quiet moan, and Kinsley doesn't say anything, so I hope she didn't hear.

"Fine. Y'all have fun. I still love you, Beck."

"I know," he tells her, my pussy soaking wet as he finger-fucks me. "Kinda busy, though. My hands are all tied up. Gonna let you go now." Beckett meets my eyes and doesn't give her a chance to say anything before he ends the call. Then he moves forward and devours my mouth.

His phone rings, and he groans, removing his fingers but still teasing my clit.

"Okay. Damn. I'll be there in"—his eyes meet mine—"ten minutes?"

I nod and whisper, "I only need five."

He grins, then the call ends. "I don't have much time. My lesson arrived early."

Beckett removes his fingers from my panties and places them into his mouth. "Fuck, I need that pussy."

I grab his hand, leading him inside the house. Right now,

it's empty, though a few pieces of furniture the Whitleys left behind are still here. I take zero time sliding my leggings and panties down as he bends me over the back of the couch.

Beckett's cock is long and hard, and he enters me hard and fast. I'm wet for him, horny and hot, and he breathlessly fucks me into oblivion.

Reaching around, he plays with my clit, slamming his cock into me with earth-shattering force. I groan out his name.

"Harder," I demand as he takes me from behind.

My ass slaps against his legs, and the sounds fill the silence of the big empty house. We'll eventually christen every room in this place—one of our bucket list items before the grand opening in six weeks.

He grunts, pumping hard and fast into me, nearly ripping me in two. The air is stuffy, and beads of sweat form on my brow. My back arches, and I'm unable to hold the orgasm in any longer as he fucks me to oblivion. His warmth fills me, and hot cum drips down my leg. The sensation of having him as mine still overwhelms me, especially in moments like this.

"Let me see, sweetheart." He looks at our arousal mixed. As I watch him, I place a finger inside my tight walls, then place it into my mouth. "That's us."

His lips slam against mine, and we're lost in each other again. The only thing that pulls us away is his buzzing phone. "Shit, I gotta go. Harrison is gonna beat my ass if I don't show up soon. Our next lesson already arrived. Overly punctual people are annoyin'."

"You ain't gotta tell me that. I know. Kinsley is one of the most punctual people I know. What time will you be done trainin'?"

"Right before dark. But you should meet me in the barn. I'd love to fuck on Harrison's tidy little desk."

I snicker. "What about the hay loft?"

"Girl, you're playin' with fire."

"And you know I'm not afraid to get burned."

He kisses me one last time. "I love you."

"I love you, too." I grab his ass as he walks away, and I quickly clean myself up with some paper towels from the kitchen.

I lean against the counter, envisioning what this place will be like when it's full of families. We'll be able to give them a true West Texas experience.

A smile touches my lips because never in my life did I imagine all of my dreams would come true at the same time. I have my B&B, and I have Beckett Valentine.

I'm so lucky, and if Kinsley's woo is true, and she manifested it all, I owe her everything. I've won the life lottery. Now it's her turn.

I'm not one to play matchmaker, but I will if I need to. One day, she'll find someone who makes her just as happy as Beckett makes me. She's sugar and spice and everything nice. At times like this, I wish I had a brother for her to marry.

I suck in a deep breath and smile. As she said, everything works out how it should, and now I'm finally a believer.

24

BECKETT

*S*ummer and I stand on the porch of the bed-and-breakfast behind a bright red ribbon. All of our friends and family crowd in front of the house, smiling at us.

Radiant pink and blue flowers line the cobblestone pathway that leads straight to us. Summer eventually gave up and hired Vera to landscape the place. She was happy to design it and even used her employee discount at the nursery to help save money. Each day, she stops by, tends to the plants, and even sings to them. Sometimes I wonder how she's my sister because she's too nice.

With a kind smile, Mayor Martinez hands Summer a giant pair of golden scissors.

"I'd like to congratulate you personally, Ms. Jones. This will be a fine establishment for the citizens and visitors of Valentine."

Summer gives him a genuine smile, her eyes twinkling like the stars at night. "Thank you. But, I couldn't have done it without my boyfriend and the rest of the Valentine family, along with my own, who pitched in and made this dream a reality."

My girl reaches over and interlocks her fingers with mine. I lift her hand and place a kiss on her knuckles. A hint of blush touches her cheeks, and I love that she still responds to my touch. I hope she always does.

"Please, do us the honor, Ms. Jones."

Summer smiles up at me, then her parents before opening the oversized scissors and snipping the ribbon. It falls away, and the crowd erupts into applause.

The band Harrison hired begins playing in the background, and the scents of the smoked barbecue Summer's family is serving wafts throughout the air.

Today, we're celebrating all the hard work it took Summer to make this dream a reality. I'm proud as hell of her.

"Y'all get together for a picture. Goin' on the front page of the Sunday paper." Kinsley smiles wide, holding up a fancy camera and snapping a few pictures.

Summer and I walk around the crowd, exchanging hugs and hellos with every one of my family members and hers. When we finally have a chance alone on the dance floor, she kisses me.

"What was that for?" I rest my hands in her back pockets as we sway to country music.

"For being you."

I smirk. "Yeah, yeah. Pretty sure you hated me for being me for as long as I can remember."

"Hated you?" She playfully gasps. "I was just annoyed that I couldn't have you."

"You've got me now, so whatcha gonna do about it?" I twist her around, then bring her back to my body.

"Keep you forever."

"One day"—I lean in and whisper in her ear—"I'm gonna make you my wife."

A soft smile meets her lips. "Can you not wait until we're fifty?"

I inhale the flowery scent of her hair. "You want kids?"

"Maybe after I've fully enjoyed my husband."

I pull away, placing a kiss on her forehead. "Good answer. But gotta warn ya. My mama is already demandin' grandchildren."

Summer looks over her shoulder at my mom and dad sitting in lawn chairs in front of the makeshift stage. "She can wait. As long as Harrison keeps actin' like a baby, she won't even notice."

This causes me to burst out into laughter. A few people look at me, but I don't care.

"Have I told you how much I love you today?"

"Yep, when you were between my legs this mornin'."

"Are you always so used to talkin' about…you know what… in public?"

Now she's the one laughing. "You can blame your sister for that one."

"She's somethin' else." I find Kinsley with her camera, taking photographs for the article.

Summer nods. "Yeah, but ya gotta love her. That's one thing that I'm lookin' forward to, though. Being Kinsley's sister, officially."

"Makes me think she's the only reason you started datin' me."

Summer gives me a pointed look and fists the bottom of my polo. "She's the only reason I gave you a chance."

"Then I guess I owe her a thank-you."

"She's already requested to be the godparent of our firstborn."

I playfully shake my head. "Isn't being an aunt enough?"

"You know, I said the same thing. She said no. Because our kid will have four other aunts. She said it's not special."

"Are you talkin' about me?" Kinsley's wearing her million-dollar smile.

"Yep. I guess you get to be the godparent to our kid."

She gasps and turns to Summer. "Oh my God, are you pregnant?"

"No, no. I'm not ready for all of that."

"Summer's pregnant?" I hear my mother say.

Summer glares at Kinsley. "You do realize this is how rumors get started."

Kinsley clears her throat. "Attention, everyone! Summer is absolutely *not* pregnant!"

"Wow, you are somethin' else, aren't ya?" I tell her.

Summer's face is bright red, and I find it adorable that she's embarrassed.

"Not yet!" I add, and she playfully swats at me as everyone laughs.

"I'm *officially* mortified. Thank you both. I'll have to make sure to return the favor as *soon* as *possible*."

I wrap my arms around my girl and place a chaste kiss on her lips. She looks up at me with love and admiration, the same way I look at her. There are times when I can't believe this is my life. That I'm dating the woman of my dreams, and I can promise one thing, I won't be letting her go.

Mayor Martinez walks over, congratulating us once again.

"New training facility going up back there?" he asks, looking at the steel structure.

"Yes, sir." I wear a proud smile.

"Smart idea. I wish you both many years of success. Also, I heard a rumor…"

My brow pops up with anticipation.

"I heard Cash may be moving back to town and opening an equestrian veterinary office right here."

I chuckle. "Not a rumor, sir. Just reality."

His grin widens. "Fantastic. Valentine needs a local who's for locals. The last time I had to get my horse looked at, it was an all-day excursion."

Summer nods. "That's true. We're gonna have our own little empire right here."

"If you ever need anything, ya know where to find me. Congratulations once again."

He holds out his hand and takes mine in a firm shake, then shakes Summer's.

"Thank you," we say in unison.

The crowd slowly peels away, and before everyone leaves, Summer finds her mom and dad. She grabs my hand, pulling me with her.

"What do you think about the place?" Summer looks between her parents for their blessing. They're beaming with pride.

"You did such a great job, sweetie." Mr. Jones pats her on the back.

"And the landscaping." There's amazement in her mama's tone, and I hold back laughter. Holding back a smirk, however, is impossible.

She swats at me. "Vera helped."

"Of course she did. That young lady is so talented. You know, she told me exactly what type of hangin' plant I should get for the porch."

"And it's still alive," her father adds.

"Thanks for the burn, Dad. Appreciate that."

He chuckles, then meets my eyes. "You keepin' her in check?"

"Yes, sir, as best as I can."

He understands how stubborn Summer can be. Hell, we all do.

"We're very proud of you kids. You've done an amazing job gettin' the house renovated. That barn you got back there is mighty fine. Need to get me one of those built on my property."

"Yes, sir. I know a guy who won't charge ya an arm and a leg when you're ready."

"Give me his contact info. Not now, though. Stop by sometime next week, and we'll chat."

There's a hint of something in his tone.

"Yes sir."

He holds out his hand, and I take it. His grasp is firm. "Next week, then."

"Well, we're headed to the house." Her mama holds out her arms, and Summer falls into them. Then she squeezes me tight. "Now y'all don't be workin' too hard, ya hear?"

"Yes, ma'am," I answer.

When they're out of earshot, Summer turns to me. "Is my dad gonna kick your ass or somethin'?"

"Shit, I hope not. He nearly crushed my hand when he shook it."

She laughs. "He's probably gonna threaten ya."

I watch them walk to his truck. "Ain't no big thang. I've not done anything wrong unless lovin' you is a sin. And baby girl, if it is, I don't wanna be right."

Summer rolls her eyes. "Way too cheesy for my taste."

"Hey, you love cheese."

"On my food, not from my boyfriend."

"Hey, say that again."

"What? You like it when I call you my boyfriend?"

I nod, pulling her in for a kiss.

"Don't get too used to it, though." She raises a brow.

"Oh, I won't. 'Cause one day, I'm gonna make you my wife. Then I'll get upgraded to husband."

"More like husbutt." Kinsley walks up wearing a cheeky grin.

"Why are you in such a good mood?" Summer asks.

Kinsley shrugs. "Nothing like christening in an old house."

My mouth falls open. "You didn't."

Moments later, I see Luca walk out the front door.

Summer gives Kinsley a high five.

I shake my head. "I take back all the times I said we were anything alike. You're more like him." I point over at Harrison, who has three ladies surrounding him.

Kinsley chuckles. "Nah, I can't bag 'em like he does. Somehow, he got the Valentine charm. You wouldn't know about that, though. I think it skipped you, too."

Summer snorts.

"Hey! I'm charming!" However, I know I'm the butt of the joke.

I lean in and whisper in Summer's ear. "Keep it up and tonight I'll make sure to play dirty."

"I love the sound of that."

"Oh God. I don't want to know what you just said." Kinsley turns and looks at Luca, and I see something flicker in her eyes.

"You like him?" I meet her gaze.

My sister shrugs. "He's great. But we're just seein' what happens, ya know?"

Summer's face contorts. "Kins. I warned you about this."

"I know. I like him. Is it love? Not sure. The sex is fuckin' great, though. Not ever gonna complain about gettin' dicked down."

"Okay, that's enough." I shake my head and back away. "Nope. Not gonna listen to that."

"Puh-lease." Kinsley laughs. "Like your locker room talk with Harrison is any better. Give me a break."

"Speakin' of breaks, you know I'm gonna break that dude's neck if he breaks your heart."

"Nothin' is getting broken, not his neck and not my heart. I'm good. Great. For the first time in a long time, I'm in a happy place, ya know? A part of me still believes in love. The candle ain't completely blown out."

"Yet." I grab Summer's hand and interlock my fingers with hers. She stands close, rubbing her thumb against mine.

Kinsley sighs. "Yet."

"Is he still goin' back to New York?" Summer squeezes my fingers.

"Yeah. He's leavin' in October. Told me this mornin'. I

can't stop him from pursuing his dreams, ya know? We're not exclusive or anything."

"But you want to be." I wait for her to confirm, but she doesn't.

"That would just complicate things." She forces a smile. "But enough about me and my shitty datin' life. How are things with you two? Fuckin' every morning and night still? Enjoy it while you can. That wears off. The honeymoon stage and all that. But then again, you two are sick for each other, so who knows. I truly love that for y'all."

"Thanks, sis." I release Summer's hand and give Kinsley a hug. "I was serious about breakin' his neck, though."

She laughs, then pushes away. "Just worry about yourself."

Summer wraps her in a tight hug.

"I'm happy for you, SumSum."

"Ugh, don't you start calling me that, too. I only accept it when you're drunk because you don't know better."

"Does bein' cum drunk count?"

"Jesus!" I yell, and my parents look at me. "Loves the little children." I force a smile. "Kins. You're too much."

"She says things like that for the shock value." Summer laughs, and Kinsley shrugs. "Or maybe I'm desensitized."

"The last one. Definitely, the last one," I tell her.

Luca comes over and wraps his arm around Kinsley's waist. She leans into him and looks at him with googly eyes. He kisses her sweetly and says hello, then they walk away together.

Summer and I turn to each other.

"She looks at him like she used to look at Hayden."

"I know." I run my fingers through my hair. "This is going to be bad when he leaves, isn't it?"

"The absolute worst. One of two things will happen. Either she'll be mopey and sad, or she'll go on a fuck spree to get him out of her head."

"And this is exactly why I worry about her." Summer and I

walk down the cobblestone sidewalk toward the bed-and-breakfast.

"You shouldn't worry about her. If any woman can take care of herself, it's Kins."

"You're right. But it doesn't mean she's immune to heartache."

EPILOGUE

*T*he bed-and-breakfast was busy today, and I couldn't be happier even if I'm exhausted. Beckett's sister Remi was tired of her online personal assistant job, and I offered her a position working for me. Since she's basically family, I know I can trust her to run the night shifts. Plus, she loves to read and watch YouTube, so she's been catching up on all of her old favorites.

I drive past the concrete foundation for Cash's veterinary clinic, noticing the progress, then head home. Beckett and I have been discussing our future a lot more lately. Since we've gotten ahead on the mortgage for the ranch, we've talked about building a house of our own.

However, it feels like a very grown-up thing to do. The thought alone makes me laugh.

It's early September, and I turn thirty next month, right around Halloween. But my mama loves Summer, hence the name. I'm more of an autumn lover myself. Something is special about a new season, a slower time, with bonfires, crispy leaves, and lower temperatures. Especially after dealing with 100+ degrees not too long ago.

I park in front of the house, wondering where Beckett is. Once I'm inside, I drop my keys onto the table by the door and glance at the picture of me, Beckett, and Kinsley. We were thick as thieves as kids, and I'm glad Beckett and I found our way to each other as adults.

"Beckett?" I call out, wandering through the house. Just because his truck isn't here doesn't mean he isn't. The man walks or rides horses, four-wheelers, or side-by-sides everywhere.

There's no answer.

When I go to the kitchen to grab some water, I find a fresh bouquet of yellow roses and see a note lying on the counter. I pick it up, noticing it's written in Beckett's handwriting.

"Meet me at the pond. The bonfire is getting lit this weekend. Left a four-wheeler for you by the side of the house. Oh, I brought dinner."

I chuckle. He's ridiculous, but he also knows I can't pass up a chance to snuggle by the fire under the stars. New constellations are rising, and new objects will be up in the night sky for me to learn. Before I head out, I quickly jump into the shower and wash away the day, then put on some comfortable clothes. I grab an extra blanket, just in case it gets cold, then I leave.

The drive down the trail in the late evening is one of my favorites, especially during this time of year, when I can see the seasons changing. Bright orange leaves hang on for dear life, and crispy brown ones crumble beneath the tires. A smile touches my lips as I give it more gas, hauling ass to the clearing in the distance.

The trail of smoke reaches up toward the open sky—a signal the fire is burning and Beckett's waiting for me. When I finally arrive, he turns around, greeting me with his boyish grin. He's wearing a hoodie and jeans, and his hair is a mess on his head.

"Hey, baby." He comes over to me, greeting me with a greedy kiss.

"Hi." I get out between little nibbles. "I've missed you, too."

I glance behind him, seeing a nice blanket on the ground and a picnic basket. There's also a bottle of wine. "What's the occasion?" I grin, fisting his shirt and pulling him against me.

He playfully gasps. "You forgot?"

I search his face.

"It's the four-month-a-versary of me tasting that sweet pussy, right there, in that very spot."

I burst into laughter, and he captures me with his mouth again.

"You're too much." I shake my head, and he leads me there.

"Oh my goodness, you sprinkled the blanket with pumpkin cut-outs made of material. Aw, how cute."

"I'd do anything for my fall queen."

I smile wide. "I'm the winter queen, too."

"I'm aware. There were times when you were cold as ice."

I playfully swat at him, but I miss. He's too fast.

"Milady." He holds out his hand, helping me down.

I sit cross-legged, taking in the heat from the fire, watching the logs burn bright.

"Ya hungry?" Beckett joins me on the blanket and grabs the basket. Then he takes the cork out of the wine and pours some into a cup.

I take a drink. "Gah, that's good. Reminds me of underage drinking and old country music."

He smirks. "Cheers to Deanna Carter, wherever she is."

We tap our cups together and laugh, then listen to the fire crackling. "What's for dinner?"

He pulls out two plastic bowls with lids, spoons, and then a container with cornbread. "Chili night."

"Mmm, my favorite."

Beckett laughs. "I swear you say that every single time we eat."

"I love food. Well, I love the food that I love, and that's why I always order the same things. I know what to expect."

"Kinda like being with you." He throws a wink my way.

"Not sure if that's a burn or a compliment."

"Total compliment." He hands me a napkin, then leans forward and kisses me on my cheek. "You feel like home, SumSum."

I grin. "Inside and out?"

"Abso-fucking-lutely."

I dip my spoon inside the bowl and take a big bite. It's still warm, and it hits the spot. "I'm envious that you know how to cook so well."

"You're cute. I've only got a handful of recipes." He reaches for his wine.

"And I've got you. So I guess I still win." I laugh, breaking off a piece of cornbread and dipping it into the chili.

We talk about our day and our plans for tomorrow while we eat. When we're finished, Beckett loads everything back into the basket. "I'm gonna put this up. Wanna add more wood to the fire?"

"Sure." I stand and stretch. My feet nearly fell asleep sitting like that.

Beckett walks to the four-wheeler he drove here, and I move toward the stack of logs he has off to the side. It's got a tarp over it just in case it rains. I peel back the plastic and grab two big pieces.

Glittery red sparks fly high into the night as I toss one inside the fire. Then I throw the other in, crashing it into the pile, and it does the same. The fire licks up the sides of the fresh wood, and I hear it pop and crackle. When I turn around to see what's taking Beckett so long, he's down on one knee, holding a black box.

I swallow hard, covering my heart in my chest.

Goose bumps course over my skin, and excitement fills me.

"Summer Jones." Beckett smiles up at me, opening the box. Inside is a solitair diamond ring that belonged to my grandmother. My mouth falls open, and an overwhelming amount of emotions overtake me. He spoke to my daddy to get that ring, a symbol of acceptance from my family. Permission for him to take me away. The moment I see the ring, tears well on the edges of my eyes.

"I've been waitin' my whole life to make you mine. You're my other half, Summer, and I want to spend the rest of my days with you. Loving you. Will you be a Valentine and become my wife?"

I drop to my knees and topple on top of him. "Yes. Yes!" I kiss him, my tongue sliding against his. "I love you. I can never say it enough. You're my favorite."

Beckett kisses me again and again. "I love you, sweetheart. And I'll never get tired of hearing it."

BECKETT

I slide the ring onto her trembling hand, then peer into her eyes. I place my palm on her cheek, and we kiss until our lips are swollen, barely able to breathe.

Falling back on the blanket, Summer unbuckles my belt and slides down my jeans. She removes her bottoms and then straddles me, taking in every inch and claiming me as hers.

I roll her over and hover above her, swiping her hair from her face as I slowly enter her. As she digs her heels into my ass, she pants and moans, forcing me forward.

"Yes, Beck. Yes."

I slide deep into her, my emotions boiling to the surface as her pussy squeezes my cock so tight I nearly see stars.

"You're so beautiful." I lightly brush my lips against hers.

I hold her close as we make love under the Milky Way to the sounds of the crickets and popping fire. There's no rush, and we enjoy every damn second. Summer's going to be my wife, and I'm almost tempted to pinch myself to make sure I'm not dreaming.

I'm so in love with this woman in ways I never imagined were possible.

She made me believe that a happily ever after was possible, even for a country boy like me.

After we've lost ourselves in each other and the orgasm shreds through us, we nearly fall asleep in each other's arms.

I stir, realizing how late it's getting. "We should go, sweetheart."

"Yeah. I'm just so comfortable."

"I got you, baby. Leave the other four-wheeler here, and we'll drive mine back."

She nods as I stand, holding out my hand and helping her up. She takes it and hops onto the back of the four-wheeler. Quickly, I grab the bucket, fill it with pond water, then douse the fire. Then we leave. She wraps her arms around my waist and holds me all the way home.

When we walk inside, Summer is all smiles.

"I have to call Kins and tell her the good news."

"Yeah." I nod. "Don't want her to find out second. Thankfully, Harrison has continued to keep our dating secret safe."

Summer laughs. "I told her Harrison knew first."

My eyes go wide. "I had to work for him for an entire month to keep that secret."

"It was later. She didn't care. But this? She'd divorce me as a best friend."

Summer sits on the couch, and I join her as she calls Kinsley on speaker.

The phone rings and rings, and right before her voicemail picks up, Kinsley answers, and she's breathless.

"Hey! Sorry. What's goin' on?"

"Everything okay?" Summer immediately detects something.

"No. I'm fuckin' pissed."

I make a face, and so does Summer. She looks at me and puts her finger over her mouth.

"What's up?"

"It's Hayden." It sounds like her teeth are clenched when she says his name.

Yeah, she's pissed.

"What about him?"

There's a long pause. "He's back in town."

Summer's eyes go as wide as mine. "What? Is he just visitin'?"

"No. He's back for good."

I don't know what to say, and going by the silence, neither does Summer.

"I'm sorry," Kinsley says. "Anyway, you called me. Everything okay?"

Summer smiles. "I wanted to tell you that…"

"We're engaged," we say together.

Kinsley squeals with excitement. "For real? This is the best news I've heard all day! Congrats, you two! Oh my God. I'm so happy for you. Like, this is incredible. Oh, I'm the maid of honor, right?"

Summer laughs. "Oh my goodness, of course."

"Well, it seems like we have a wedding and a funeral to plan," Kinsley says.

"Uh, *just* a wedding," I interrupt.

"Oh no, see, that's where you got it wrong, big brother. Hayden has it coming."

"Don't go startin' battles you can't finish," Summer warns.

"A battle?" She lets out choked laughter. "Bless his heart. This is war."

THE END

This concludes Beckett and Summer's story, but I wrote an exclusive bonus scene just for you!
https://lyraparish.com/beckettandsummer

* * *

Want to know what happens between Kinsley and Hayden?
Continue the Valentine Texas Series in *Spill the Sweet Tea*!
https://geni.us/spillthesweettea

ACKNOWLEDGMENTS

Now, I'm really bad at thanking people individually, so if I've forgotten anyone, it's not on purpose. Please forgive me in advance. I haven't written personalized acknowledgments in about seven years, so buckle up, this one might be long.

First of all, big thanks to my hubby, Will Young/Deep Sky Dude, who has listened to me talk about these characters and the precarious positions I left them in when it was time to stop writing. You're my favorite and always will be. I love you so much. I couldn't do this without your support and encouragement. You're always there when I need you the most, and I couldn't imagine spending forever with anyone else. You really are the MVP of this operation.

Super big thank you to Rachel Brookes for forever being my 1.0 since 2014 and for always cheering me on through the good and the bad. Everyone needs a Rach in their life, someone who can find the positive in all things. I hope to be the same cheerleader for you. Even if I gave up writing tomorrow, I know for a fact we'd still be friends, no matter what. ILYSM! Seattle? Greece? The world is our oyster.

Thank you to JS Cooper for being a true friend and for lending an car. I owe you several bottles of wine and big, squishy Southern hugs. And to Gwyn McNamee, but I know you're not really a hugger, so an extra bottle of wine for you. Oh, and I will always mention D. Kelly because she's like my big sister and has helped me through some of the roughest times in my life. Please write the island books!

Can't go on without thanking Teralyn Mitchell for volunteering to read Bless Your Heart before it was sent to edits and for giving me the feedback I needed. Thank you for being a night owl cheerleader and for all of your support over the years.

A SUPER big thank you to Dee Garcia at Black Widow Designs. OMG. Ma'am, you're magical and so uber-talented. I know I've told you this so many times, but please don't forget me when you're booked to the brim. I don't think this book could've been published without your artistic touch, and I will forever be grateful for you and your ability to nail it *every* single time. She's mine, y'all!

Thanks to Wander Aguiar and team for providing me with a photo that just screamed BLESS YOUR HEART. As authors, we sometimes search for hours, days, and even weeks for the right photo, and yours are just chef's kiss. Makes my job easy. Big shoutout to the cover model Lachy, because I just don't think it would be the same without him on the front of this book.

Thanks to my amazing PA, Breanna Kelly, for being amazing. Thank you for being there when I needed you. I'm so grateful to have you on my dream team.

Also, thanks to all the bookish influencers who gave me a chance. You're the bomb(dot)com!

Thanks to Jenny Sims for being an editor extraordinaire and for sticking with me since 2015 and to Amanda Cuff for having eagle eyes. The book just wouldn't be where it is today without both of you.

Can't end this without giving a shout-out to Candi Kane PR and Give Me Books Promotions for helping spread the word. And a big thank you to all the writers who joined me online and sprinted with me. You guys motivate me to be better and do better.

And I'll end this by giving a big thank you to my Dad. He was VERY proud that I wrote romance and was a published author and told people at the most inappropriate times. He instilled that fighting spirit in me. I miss him every single day, and I keep going even when it's hard because he wouldn't accept anything else. Dad always told me not to give up and to keep going. And I'll continue to make him proud even if he's not here to witness it. Love you, Dad! I'm still keeping all my promises.

KEEP IN TOUCH

Want to say up-to-date with all things Lyra Parish? Make sure to join her newsletter. You'll get special access to cover reveals, teasers, and giveaways.

lyraparish.com/newsletter

Social Media:
Tikok & Instagram: **@lyraparish**
facebook.com/lyraparishauthor

ABOUT LYRA PARISH

Lyra Parish is a hopeless romantic who enjoys creating characters who eventually find love. She likes to write Texas small-town romances (because she's a 5th-generation Texan) and romantic suspense. When she isn't immersed in fictional worlds, you can find her on Youtube chatting about her self-publishing journey or podcasting about romance books. Lyra's a Virgo who loves coffee, the great outdoors, authentic people, and living her very best life with her hubby. You may or may not know her from when she co-wrote under the USA Today Bestselling pen name Kennedy Fox.

Made in United States
Orlando, FL
17 June 2023

34239100R00148